The C
A Psyc

CW00448204

By

April Fernsby

www.aprilfernsby.com

Copyright 2019 by April Fernsby

Front Cover by www.coverkicks.com[1]

Proofreading by Paula Proofreader[2]

This is a work of fiction and any resemblance to any person living or dead is purely coincidental.

---

1. http://www.coverkicks.com

2. https://paulaproofreader.wixsite.com/home

Chapter 1

I felt Peggy staring at me from across the café. I knew what she was thinking. I was thinking the same. It had been weeks since I'd had a psychic vision warning me about a murder. I was relieved about that, but also a little worried. Had I lost my gift? Or were people in this town behaving themselves and not killing each other?

I gave Peggy a little wave to show everything was okay at this side of the café.

The café had closed for the day and we were getting ready for another one of our craft evenings. It was going to be a cross stitch event. I knew barely anything about that art, but Peggy was an expert. My elderly friend and neighbour was an expert in almost everything craft-wise.

Peggy frowned at my wave, and then made her way towards me, weaving around the café tables. "What was that wave for?" she asked. "Have you had a vision? What did you see? Is someone about to get murdered? In here? Tonight? Karis, that would be very inconvenient. I've set the display up and everything."

I held my hands up in defence. "I haven't had a vision. And even if I had, you know I can't control them and what happens in them."

She gave me a long look. "I'm not convinced. You've got a shifty look in your eyes. Why? If it's nothing to do with a vision, then what are you keeping from me?"

Peggy knew me so well. She had lived next door to Mum and Dad for years, and known me since birth. Since Dad had died, and Mum had moved into a care home, I was the one who lived in the family home now.

It was impossible to lie to Peggy. I had tried over the years, but failed.

"Oh, it's nothing," I said. I could feel the weight of her stare as she waited for me to admit the truth. "Okay. It's that cross stitch thing you asked me to do. I know you wanted me to finish it for tonight, but I haven't."

"Why not? It's only a little one. Just a couple of roses in a vase. It's not complicated." She shook her head at me. "I wanted to show the group tonight what an inexperienced beginner with no artistic talent could do."

"Is that an insult?"

She chuckled. "Perhaps, but I didn't mean it as one. I know you've been busy in the café all day. But you do far too much. And your sister is just as bad."

I glanced towards the kitchen where my sister Erin was. "I know. I wish she'd take it easy. I know she's having regular check-ups, but that doesn't mean she has to continue working so hard."

"She's pregnant, not ill." Peggy looked towards the kitchen too. "I worry just as much, though. But you can't force her to rest. You know how stubborn she is." She put her attention back on me. "How far have you got with the cross stitch? You have made a start on it, haven't you?"

"A little."

"What do you mean by that?"

"I've threaded the needle."

Peggy's eyes widened. "Is that it?"

I shrugged. "It's a start."

She shook her head again. "Have you brought it with you?"

"I have. It's in my bag."

"Good. You can work on it while I run the class. Then at the end of the evening, you can show me what you've done. Okay?" She gave me that stern look of hers which I knew so well.

"Okay."

"You'll enjoy it. It's a very relaxing hobby."

"It doesn't feel like it, not with you going on at me about it."

She was instantly contrite. "Karis, I'm sorry. You know what I get like at these craft evenings. I get very tetchy. I want everyone to have a good time. Then they'll leave good reviews on our website. Am I being too bossy?"

I smiled. "A bit. But I still love you. Show me the display you've set up over there. Are those all your cross stitch pictures? I didn't know you'd made so many."

"I like to keep myself busy. Follow me. You might even get inspired to take on a bigger project yourself, once you've mastered the basics."

As we walked over to the far area where the craft evening was to be held, there was a knock at the main café door.

Peggy muttered, "I hope that's not someone wanting a cup of tea. The café's closed."

I looked towards the door and saw a woman smiling widely at us through the upper glass panel. She was holding a cardboard box full of things I couldn't identify from where I was standing.

Peggy said, "Oh, it's Anita! She's a bit early. You know Anita Hart, don't you? She runs Hart's Haberdashery. It's been in her family for years." Without waiting for my answer, Peggy went over to the door and opened it.

Anita bustled in. She was in her late fifties or early sixties. She had a harassed look about her. "Peggy, sorry for turning up early. I can't stay long. Mum's had one of her turns again."

"Poor love. Have you sent for the doctor?"

"No. Mum doesn't want one. You know what she's like. She said I should stay for the craft event here, but I'd only worry about her. I've brought my supplies like we agreed. Where can I put them?" She held the box up.

I took the box from Anita and said, "Hi. I don't think we've met. I'm Karis. I run this café with my sister."

She returned my smile. "I know who you are. Peggy talks about you and your sister all the time. I was sorry to hear about your divorce, but I'm not surprised. That ex-husband of yours sounds a right piece of work. And the things he said to you! And the women he met up with all the time! Isn't that what you said, Peggy?"

I gave Peggy an accusing look. She had the decency to look embarrassed. She said, "Now, Anita, we haven't got time for gossip. What goodies have you brought us?"

I put the box on the nearest table and took a closer look at the contents.

Anita tapped the box and said, "I've got a variety of cross stitch kits here, Peggy. Are you sure you don't mind selling them tonight? I feel a bit cheeky asking you to do that, especially since I won't be here."

"I don't mind at all, Anita. Your kits are always a bargain. Let's have a proper look at them. I'll probably buy a few myself. You know I can't resist them."

Peggy pulled some of the kits out. There were images of flowers, houses and country scenes on the front of them. I looked closer at some smaller ones and took one out which had an image of the Eiffel Tower on it. I didn't know why, but I had to have it.

I said, "I'll buy this one. Have you got any more like it?"

"I have." Anita dug into the box and pulled a few more out. "How about this one of the Colosseum in Rome? And this one of that building in Greece? The Acropolis. I think that's what it is."

I took the kits. Excitement rose in me. "These are perfect, thank you."

Peggy's voice was slightly too high as she asked, "Karis, why do you want them? You haven't finished your first project yet."

I knew what she was getting at. She was worried I was getting a psychic vision concerning these kits. She was right to be worried. I was starting to get a weird feeling about them. They were important to me, but I didn't know why.

I said casually, "I like the look of them. Lorrie and I are planning on doing some travelling to Europe soon. I might make these as a gift for her." My excuse sounded feeble, and I'm sure Peggy's worries had now doubled. I explained to Anita,

"Lorrie is my daughter and we don't see each other as much as I'd like to."

Anita smiled. "I know how important family is. You can have those for free, Karis. I've had them in the shop for years, but no one's ever been interested in them."

"Oh, I must pay," I argued. "How much are they?" I turned the packets over to look at the price. My eyebrows shot up when I did. "How much? That can't be right."

Anita laughed. "Those prices are from years ago. I just can't shift them. You'd be doing me a favour by taking them off my hands."

I gave her a small nod of thanks. I couldn't take my eyes off the kits. Why were they so important? Was I about to have a vision? I waited for the familiar feeling to arrive, but nothing happened. I was aware of Peggy and Anita talking, so I focused my attention on them instead.

Anita had just handed Peggy a wrapped package. "Here you are, Peggy. I framed it for you. It looks amazing. You worked really hard on it."

"With your help," Peggy said with a smile. "I'll be sure to tell everyone later about the new service you offer."

"What's that?" I asked, nodding at the package.

"A secret project I've been working on," Peggy explained. "I'll reveal all later. Are you sure you can't stay for a while, Anita? Not even for a quick cuppa?"

"I can't, sorry. I'd better get back to Mum. Let me know how your evening goes. If any of the kits don't sell, just bring them back to me when you get the chance. Thanks again." She smiled at me. "It was nice to meet you, Karis. If you need any help with those kits, just let me know. Bye!" She gave us a swift wave before leaving the café.

My glance went to the package which Peggy was holding against her chest. I said, "Go on; tell me what's inside. You don't need to keep things secret from me."

"And you don't have to keep secrets from me. Tell me the real reason you wanted those kits. It's to do with Anita, isn't it? Did you have a vision about her? Is she about to die?" She let out a heavy sigh. "You can tell me. I can take it."

"I didn't have a vision. Honest. But I did get a funny feeling about these kits. I'm not sure why."

Peggy looked towards the café door. "Try not to have a vision about Anita. I would hate for something awful to happen to her."

"I'll do my best."

We both knew my words meant nothing. If I was supposed to get a premonition about a death, then there was nothing I could do to stop the images coming to me.

Chapter 2

Peggy was subdued as she took the box of cross stitch kits over to the craft part of the café. I was about to follow her when I felt the hairs on the back of my neck lift. My head turned towards the kitchen.

Erin! There was something wrong with her.

I dashed into the kitchen, fearing the worst. Erin was leaning over the sink and sobbing.

"Erin? What's wrong? Is it the babies?" I was at her side in a flash. I put my arm around her heaving shoulders. "Talk to me."

She turned her tear-filled face my way and gave me a wobbly smile. "It's nothing. The babies are fine. It's me. I'm being silly." She turned around and rested her hands on her stomach. She was expecting twins, and her stomach seemed to be expanding by the second.

I took her over to the table and sat her down. "Tell me what's going on."

She wiped her tears away with the back of her hand. "I love being pregnant. I don't mind getting bigger every day. And I love feeling the babies kick me. I don't even care that I have to get up fifty million times in the night to have a wee. I'm savouring every day of my pregnancy." She smiled down at her stomach.

My thoughts went to the four miscarriages she'd had. A few months ago, I'd had a vision about Erin's babies. I'd seen a healthy girl and boy. I hadn't had any visions about them since, so I assumed they were still okay. I mentally crossed my fingers and sincerely hoped they were okay.

I said gently, "And?"

She held her left hand up. "Why do my hands have to look pregnant too? Look how fat my fingers are, Karis. I didn't know they could get so fat. They look like sausages!"

I examined the sausages. I suddenly knew why she was so distressed. "You have to take your rings off, don't you? Is that why you're so upset?"

She nodded and put her hand flat on the table. "I am. I know it's silly and trivial, but these rings mean a lot to me. I remember every moment of the night Robbie proposed to me. His smiling face. His shaking hands as he held the engagement ring out to me." She laughed at the memory. "And then the wedding day. Everything about that day was perfect. I don't want to take my rings off. Ever. I'll feel disloyal to Robbie. What will he think?"

Robbie was a police officer, and one of my most favourite people in the world. Not that I've met everyone in the world, but if I had, I know Robbie would still be in my top five.

I said, "He'll think you're being sensible. He'll understand. He's one of the most understanding people I've ever met."

"I know. It's impossible to have an argument with him. Maybe I can leave my rings on for a bit longer, though. Just a day or two."

I saw how much the rings were already digging into her flesh. "Take them off now, while you still can."

She gave me a stubborn look. She put her right hand over her left as if that would make it invisible. "No. I don't want to."

I stood up. "Don't then. Let the rings cut into your skin. Let your finger get infected. Let the doctors chop it off. I don't care."

She swatted my leg. "Karis! Don't say things like that! Okay, I'll take them off. Aren't you supposed to be helping Peggy set up out there?"

"I am, but I got a feeling about you." I paused. Should I tell her about the feelings I had with the kits?

Erin stuck her hand out. "Help me up. You've got a funny look on your face. What's up? Have you had a murder vision? Who is it this time?"

I helped her up. "I haven't had a vision." I didn't expand on that. She had enough on her mind. "Have you done any of your cross stitch yet? The one Peggy gave you? I bet you haven't."

Erin lifted her chin. "That's where you're wrong. I have done it. I enjoyed it, too. I showed it to Peggy and she was most impressed. I think I'm going to do some more."

I sighed. "I haven't done mine. I'll make a start on it when Peggy's doing her talk. Let's put the food out. People will be arriving soon." I moved towards the covered trays of food which Erin had prepared, and picked a couple up.

Erin said, "I'll be with you in a minute. I'll take my rings off and put them somewhere safe, then you can stop nagging me."

I shook my head at her words. "I wasn't nagging. I never nag."

I went through to the café and placed the trays on the designated tables. The café had been renovated recently, which had brought swarms of customers in. One part of the building was used as the main café area, and the other was designed for our various craft evenings which we held. There was an upstairs area where people could go for a bit of peace and quiet. Erin's husband, Robbie, had helped with the designs and had done a marvellous job. People seemed to love our café. I know I did.

A few more visits to the kitchen, and Erin and I had everything set up. I kept looking Peggy's way and saw how busy she was. She loved organising these events and did lots of promotion online. She'd taken to the internet like a professional and even had her own blog. She'd made hundreds of friends online and kept in touch with them. I don't know where she found the energy.

A short while later, Peggy came over to us and said, "Let's unlock the door. They'll be here soon. Have we got enough food? Enough drinks?"

"We have," I confirmed.

Peggy went on, "Erin, you've done enough work today. Sit yourself down in the craft area and relax. Me and Karis will see to everything."

Erin gave her a mock salute and waddled away.

In a low voice, Peggy said to me, "Anything I need to know about? Any premonitions? I can't stop thinking about Anita. I hope she's okay."

"I haven't had any visions. Maybe I just got a strange feeling over those kits because I'll be going to some of those places soon, according to Lorrie's plans anyway."

"Yes, that could be it." She didn't look convinced. There was a knock on the door. "Here they are. I'll let them in. Don't forget about that rose cross stitch. You can do a bit while I'm giving my talk."

"I will do." I gave her a bright smile and she headed for the door.

At that moment, a weird sensation came over me. That rose cross stitch, I had to make an urgent start on it. Right now. But why?

Peggy opened the door, and chattering people stepped into the café. It was a warm night, but a cold draught headed my way. I shivered. Something awful was going to happen. I could sense it.

Chapter 3

I couldn't force the sense of unease from my mind, but I did my best to hide it as I welcomed the visitors and offered them a drink. Peggy did give me their names, but I immediately forgot them. I was vaguely aware of people carrying poster-sized packages, but as the items were covered up, I had no idea what they were. Peggy handed out welcome bags to each person, which brought smiles to everyone's faces.

Once our visitors had a drink, Peggy took them through to the craft area and told them to take a seat. I noticed Erin at the back of the room on one of the comfy sofas. I picked up a covered stool from the side of the room and headed over to her. I gently lifted her feet, pushed the stool underneath them, and then lowered her feet. She gave me a grateful smile. I noticed she was rubbing her right thumb over her empty ring finger as if searching for her rings.

"Do you need anything?" I asked. "A drink? Food? Back massage? A nap?"

She patted the seat next to her. "I want you to sit down and stop fussing. I'm capable of doing things for myself. When I get to the size of a house and can't move, then I'll have you doing everything for me. Okay?"

"Okay," I relented. I sat down.

Erin grinned and pointed to something on the table at my side. "Peggy's put your kit there. You have no excuse now."

I stared at the blank fabric. Despite my earlier urgency, I didn't want to touch it. I knew something awful would happen when I did.

Erin nudged me. "You'd better make a start. Peggy's got her eyes on you."

I reluctantly picked the fabric up. Maybe my feelings were wrong. Maybe I didn't want to make a start because I wasn't sure what I was doing. Maybe.

Peggy began speaking at the front of the room. She made a joke about something to do with cross stitch, but I didn't understand it. Everyone else did and burst into laughter. I concentrated on my work. I opened the pattern out and stared at it, hoping it would make sense. It hadn't the first time I'd looked at it, and it didn't now.

Erin tapped the sheet. "Start there. That's the easiest way to begin, and then you can work your way outwards. Pass me your fabric and I'll show you."

I did so.

"And your needle. You did put two strands of thread in your needle, didn't you? You didn't use all six in the floss, did you?"

"Floss?" I frowned. "You sound like Peggy now. You'll be talking about the count of the fabric next, whatever that is."

She rolled her eyes at me. "Let me start you off." She ran her finger over the printed pattern, then looked at the blank fabric and nodded in understanding like she was a cross stitch whisperer. Within a minute, she had made a neat line of red crosses. She handed the fabric to me and said, "There you go. It's straightforward now. Just follow the pattern."

Easy for her to say. But the strange thing was, it was easy to follow the pattern. It suddenly made sense to me as if the pattern was talking to me. I had soon completed the first petal of the rose. Feeling rather smug, I showed it to Erin. She flashed me a smile and gave her full attention back to Peggy who was still talking.

I became even more smug as I realised I could watch Peggy and do my cross stitch at the same time, if I kept glancing down at my work.

My heart filled with love at the sight of Peggy as she held up various pieces of work she'd completed over the years. She didn't have children of her own, and she was like a second mum to Erin and me. The people in front of me were hanging on to her every word. Noises of appreciation came from them at regular intervals. A sense of peace washed over me as I listened to Peggy whilst carrying on with my work. Push the needle up, over to the corner, and down it went. Each completed stitch brought me a sense of satisfaction. I was almost in a meditative state. Perhaps I would do more cross stitching.

I was brought roughly out of my blissful state by a sharp nudge in my side. Erin hissed excitedly, "This is it! This is what I've been waiting for."

"What?" I noticed everyone was fidgeting with the poster-sized items they'd brought in. Some were unwrapping them. "What's going on?"

"It's the stitch-along project." Erin's eyes were full of glee.

"The what?"

"The stitch-along. Karis, haven't you been reading Peggy's blog? Haven't you signed up for her newsletter?"

I gave her a shrug as my reply. "I've been busy."

"Too busy for your dear friend and neighbour?"

I felt a flash of guilt. "Erm, a bit. What have I missed?"

Erin's look softened. "Sorry. I didn't mean to be harsh. I know how hard you work. This café wouldn't look like this if it wasn't for you." She squeezed my hand. "Sorry."

"It's okay. Tell me about the sing-along."

"Stitch-along," she corrected. "Peggy's been sending out part of a pattern to her cross stitch followers every Friday for the last two months. It's all part of a theme. The patterns make up a whole picture, but people can add their own bits to it to make it more personal. And tonight is the big unveiling!" She clasped her hands together. "I can't wait to see what everyone's done."

I frowned. It didn't sound that exciting to me. I carried on with my work. I had finished one flower and was ready for the next one. I'd be on to the vase in no time.

At the front of the room, Peggy placed a framed picture on the table and said, "Here's my completed piece. A map of the world. I'm sure you all worked that out as soon as I sent you the first pattern!"

There were laughs and nods around the room.

Peggy pointed to the picture. "I've added my story. This bit here is Malta. It's where my hubby and I went on our honeymoon. I've attempted to stitch his face. I'm not sure I've done a good job of it. I don't think I caught his smile right. He was always smiling." Tears came to her eyes. She cleared her throat. "And this is where we went for our anniversary. All the way over to Italy. It took us hours and hours to get there, not like it does these days. Right, that's enough about me. Let's see what everyone else has brought in. Who wants to go first?"

A woman shot to her feet and declared loudly, "I will." She picked up her package and strode over to Peggy. I could have sworn I heard quiet hisses, much like you'd hear when a villain appeared in a play.

"Who's that?" I whispered to Erin.

"I don't know," she whispered back. "But Peggy doesn't like her. She's got that polite look on her face which she gives to people she can't stand."

Erin was right about that. Peggy said to the woman, "Lyla, how wonderful to see you tonight. I wasn't sure you'd make it. I thought you were off on one of your cruises again. That's what you said in your emails."

Lyla was only a few inches taller than Peggy, but she managed to look down at her as if from a great height. She gave a dismissive sniff and announced grandly, "Plans change. I couldn't get the cabin I wanted, so I changed my booking. I'll be setting sail next week instead. You can follow me online. I'll post photos." She took a step towards Peggy so that she could be in the centre more. Peggy had no option but to move out of the way.

Erin whispered to me, "I don't like her. I don't know who she is, but I don't like her one bit. Look at her standing there full of her own self-importance."

Lyla cast a condescending glance over the people in front of her. She placed her completed map on the table in front of Peggy's. She addressed her audience. "You won't be familiar with some of the places I've been to, but you can Google them later.

I couldn't even fit in all the places I've visited over the years, so I've just included the most important ones."

She proceeded to talk at length about the cruises she'd been on, and which celebrity or member of royalty she'd rubbed shoulders with. I could feel the spirits in the room deflating like a week-old party balloon. Lyla was oblivious to the effect she was having on everyone. Well, almost everyone. There was a dark-haired woman who was sitting up straight with her hands clasped together as if she couldn't contain her excitement. I could only see half of her face, but I could tell how enraptured she was with Lyla's talk. I pointed her out to Erin.

Erin raised one eyebrow and said, "It takes all sorts. I bet Lyla paid her to act like that."

Peggy's politeness wore off after a while, and she interrupted Lyla just as she was telling us about some prince she'd met in Bali. Peggy picked Lyla's map up, shoved it into Lyla's hands and said, "Thank you so much. How interesting. Who wants to go next?"

Lyla gave Peggy a sour look but didn't move.

A breathless woman came rushing into the room, holding a covered package. Her cheeks were red and her hair tousled. She mouthed an apology at Peggy and moved towards the back of the room.

Peggy beamed at her. "Maisie! I'm so glad you made it. Come up here and show us your project."

"Oh no," Maisie protested. "I've only just arrived. I don't want to push in."

"Nonsense. Lyla's finished talking about her project. Save yourself the bother of sitting down. Come on. You're more than welcome." Peggy made come-here movements with her arms.

"Oh, okay then," Maisie relented. "If you don't mind."

Erin turned to look at me, her eyes wide. She hissed, "Look at Lyla's face! If looks could kill, Maisie would be a corpse. And look at Lyla's paid fan. She's furious too. I wonder if they know Maisie, or if they just hate anyone who steals Lyla's limelight. This has suddenly got interesting." Her glance went to my fabric. She stiffened. "Karis, why did you write that?"

"What?" I strained my neck trying to get a better look at Lyla. She was sending daggers of hate towards Maisie. So was the dark-haired woman.

Erin grabbed my arm. She whispered urgently, "Karis, look at what you've done."

I looked down at my completed flowers. I blinked and frowned. Then blinked some more.

Erin traced her finger over the word I'd written above the rose. "Why did you write that?"

"I don't know. I don't remember doing it."

We stared at the word in horror: MURDER

Chapter 4

My hands shook as I tried to fold the fabric. I didn't want anyone to see that dreadful word.

"Let me." Erin took the fabric, pinned the needle in place and folded it. She put it behind her cushion. In a low voice, she asked, "Have you had a vision?"

I shook my head. My head felt light and the sounds around me faded. I said quietly, "I think I'm about to have one."

Erin's concerned face faded from my view as my psychic vision began. I could see someone, no, two people. They were standing in front of me. They were in a hall of some sort. I could hear cries and shouts coming from unseen people. Familiar smells came to me. Were they in a school? Their faces looked familiar, but young. Two girls looking at each other. One was in tears. She pleaded, "I didn't do it. I didn't. I swear." The other girl sneered and looked down at her. "I'm going to tell everyone that you did. And then they'll hate you. Just like I do."

The vision vanished in a second. I became aware of Erin holding on to my arm. "Karis? Are you alright? You were swaying about. I thought you were going to fall off the sofa. What did you see?"

I nodded in Peggy's direction. "I think I saw Maisie and Lyla when they were young, maybe in their late teens." I told Erin exactly what I'd seen.

Erin's eyes narrowed. "So, they do know each other. Although, you wouldn't think so to look at them now. Look at Lyla, she's totally ignoring Maisie. How rude."

We watched as Lyla returned to her seat, her nose high in the air as if she was smelling something disgusting. She sat next to the dark-haired woman and immediately began a heated whispered conversation. They shot occasional hate-filled looks at Maisie who had placed her project on the table.

It was clear Maisie was aware they were whispering about her, but she carried on talking about her project anyway. I hadn't caught the beginning part, but concentrated on what she was saying now.

She pointed to Australia and said shyly, "This is where I met a lovely family who showed me the local sights. They had the most amazing stories." She quickly told us one which made everyone laugh. Well, almost everyone. Lyla and her friend continued to glower at Maisie. It made me feel uncomfortable and angry. If they didn't like what Maisie was saying, then why didn't they leave?

Maisie quickly spoke about the rest of her map. She told us about the wonderful people she'd met as she'd travelled the world for her job. She didn't say what her job was. Her stories were a wonderful contrast to Lyla's, who'd only spoken about herself and who had been lucky enough to meet her.

Once Maisie had finished talking, she gave us a bashful smile, thanked Peggy and then found a seat at the back of the room.

More people came to the front to talk about their maps. As interesting as they were, I couldn't give them my full attention because Lyla and her friend had turned in their seats so that they could continue to glower at poor Maisie.

Erin noticed too and muttered, "Not in my café." She called over to Lyla, "Is there something I can help you with? Is there something fascinating at the back of this room? Do you need to take a closer look?"

Lyla flushed with anger and turned her back on us and Maisie. What was her problem?

Before I could discuss her behaviour with Erin, Peggy called out, "Now, it's time for me to reveal my own special project. I wasn't sure I would get it finished in time for tonight's event, but I did. As you know, I get most of my supplies from Anita Hart at her haberdashery shop. She's just as mad about cross stitch as we are!"

There were laughs from some of the people in front of us.

Peggy reached for the package which Anita had given her earlier. She began to unwrap it. "Anita makes her own patterns. If you go to her shop, then you've probably seen them. She helped me with something special. I wanted to make a cross stitch picture for a special person. Someone who's been through a lot recently, but she's never given up on her dreams of becoming a mum." She sent a loving look Erin's way.

Tears came to my eyes.

Erin mumbled, "Is she talking about me?"

"Of course she is," I replied. "And she hasn't finished yet."

Peggy chuckled and wiped a tear away. "I had a whole speech prepared, but I've come over all emotional. Most of you know Erin and Karis at the back there. They're like daughters to me. Erin's going to become a mum soon, and I wanted to make her something special. I gave Anita one of my most treasured photos, and she turned it into a cross stitch pattern for me. She even helped me to find the right colours for the threads. I've been working on it for weeks. And this is the result."

She took the last of the wrapping off to reveal an image of Mum, Dad, me and Erin. We were in our back garden on a summer's day. I must have been about sixteen or seventeen. Dad was linking arms with me. Mum had toddler Erin in her arms. We were laughing and smiling at the camera as if we didn't have a care in the world. I wondered if Peggy had taken that photo.

"Well?" Peggy asked. "Erin, do you like it? I thought you could hang it in your living room and show your little ones when they finally arrive. I hope you like it."

Erin burst into tears and flapped her hands at Peggy. A few incoherent words came gushing out of her mouth.

I translated. "She loves it."

Peggy was crying now. "Good. I love it too." She sniffed and put the picture down. "Where's a tissue when you need one? I thought I had one up my sleeve."

Maisie dashed forward. "Here you are, Peggy." She pressed a packet into Peggy's hand. "Shall I take that beautiful artwork over to Erin for you?"

Peggy wiped her eyes. "It's hardly artwork, but yes, thank you."

Maisie came over to us and placed the picture on Erin's lap. She said, "Can I get you anything? Cup of tea? Or a glass of water?"

Erin nodded. "Water would be lovely. Thank you."

Maisie smiled and left us.

Peggy composed herself and told everyone that Anita was offering a fifty percent discount to anyone from this group who wanted any of their photos turned into a pattern. Lots of people seemed interested in that.

Peggy called the meeting to an end. "Help yourselves to food and drink over there. Have a look at these kits on the table when you get the chance. Anita couldn't stay, but you can pay me for them. Thank you again for coming here tonight. If you want to chat with me about anything, feel free to do so."

She received a round of applause which brought colour to her cheeks. People got to their feet, including Lyla. The dark-haired woman had gone. I hadn't seen her leave.

Erin was gazing at the cross stitch picture on her lap. "Karis, look how happy we were. Do you think we should show Mum? I'm going to visit her in a few days. Should I take this with me? She might recognise us. But it might make her sad to see Dad again. She's never got over his death, has she?"

"She hasn't." I looked at the image too. Mum was in a nursing home and had stopped recognising us years ago. But every so often, there would be a glimmer of recognition in her eyes. I was ever hopeful that she'd make a recovery one day. I knew I was fooling myself, but I stubbornly refused to admit that.

Maisie returned at that moment with a glass of water for Erin. She handed it to her and said, "How far along are you? If you don't mind me asking."

"I don't mind at all," Erin replied. "I'm five months gone, and I'm having twins."

"Twins? How marvellous."

"Would you like to see my scan pictures? I keep them with me all the time." Erin reached into her pocket.

Maisie's smile was genuine. "I would love to."

I left them to it and went to check on Peggy. I noticed Lyla standing in the corner of the room giving her drink a disdainful look. The dark-haired woman was back with her. Her head was bowed and she was standing slightly behind Lyla. It looked to me as if she was standing in Lyla's shadow. That observation made me wonder how well they knew each other, and if the dark-haired one had been in Lyla's shadow for years.

I mingled amongst the guests and made sure everyone had plenty to eat and drink. Before long, it was time for people to leave. Once they had, I helped with the clearing up.

As I took a tray into the kitchen, I found Erin looking into a teapot. Her face was white.

"What's wrong?" I asked, instantly alert over her welfare.

She held the teapot up. "My rings. I put them in here. But they're gone." Her bottom lip wobbled. "Someone's stolen them."

I put the tray down and went to her side. "Are you sure you put them in there?"

"Yes. It's the fancy teapot. I never use it for tea. I keep it on the shelf for display only."

"Let's have a look around the kitchen in case you put them somewhere else."

"But I didn't. I know I put them in here. We have to tell the police. Will you do it? Will you do it now? Please." Tears ran down her face. "But don't let Robbie know. I don't want him to know how stupid I've been. I should have put them somewhere safer."

"You haven't been stupid." I put my arms around her. "We'll find out who stole them. And we'll get them back. I'll phone Seb later."

She nodded. "Thanks. You should tell him about the murder thing too. Just in case something happens."

"Murder thing?" Peggy announced behind us. "What murder thing? Karis?"

Chapter 5

I showed Peggy the rose picture I'd been working on. She didn't say anything, but her grim expression showed me what she was thinking. Her look turned even darker when Erin told her about the stolen rings.

Peggy said, "Erin, I'm so sorry. Someone from my group must have stolen them. Who else would it be? Did either of you see anyone coming in here?"

Erin shook her head. "I was sitting on the sofa for most of the night."

I added, "I was too, and then I was talking to people in the group." I paused as I remembered something. "That woman with the dark hair, the one who was sitting with Lyla; she went missing for a while."

Peggy sucked in her breath. "I know who you mean. That's Kim Webb. She's been friends with Lyla for years, since they were at school. Although, I don't think friends is the right word. Doormat would be a better one. Lyla treats Kim like dirt and yet, Kim can't see that. Wherever Lyla goes, Kim's not far behind."

"If it was Kim who stole the rings, then why would she do it?" I asked.

"Perhaps it's got something to do with your vision," Erin suggested.

"Vision? What vision?" Peggy asked. She gave me an accusing look. "Karis, nothing happens to you for ages, and then all this happens in the same night."

There was no point telling her, yet again, that I couldn't control my visions. Instead, I told her what I'd seen.

Peggy nodded. "Interesting. So Lyla and Maisie know each other. But they didn't let on about that tonight. Mind you, if I saw Lyla out and about, I'd cross the street to avoid her. Well, you saw what she was like tonight. She loves being the centre of attention."

"What do you know about Maisie?" I asked.

"Not much. Her full name is Maisie Abbot. She got in touch about a month ago and said she was moving here. She wanted to get to know people more, and said she was interested in all sorts of crafts. I told her about this cross stitch evening, and she was eager to join in. She said she used to do cross stitch when she was young. She was looking forward to this evening, but she was worried too. I got the impression she was the nervous type."

"I like her," Erin said. "She's kind and thoughtful. And a good listener. I don't like the idea of Lyla being mean to her, even if it was in the past."

"Well, there's nothing we can do about that now," Peggy surmised. "And there's not much we can do about this murder warning. Or is there? I could email everyone and ask for their thoughts on tonight's event. And if they reply, I know they're still alive." Her shoulders dropped. "And if they don't reply, well, I don't know what I'll do."

"You don't need to do anything," I said. "I'll get in touch with Seb. He takes my visions seriously. And I'll tell him about Erin's rings. He can make discreet enquiries without Robbie finding out."

Erin and Peggy shared a look, both of them smiling a little.

"What's wrong with you two?" I asked.

Peggy chuckled. "Your eyes went all misty when you talked about DCI Sebastian Parker. You like him. Admit it."

I shrugged. "He's okay. He's a good friend."

"Pah! He's more than a good friend," Peggy said. "At least, he wants to be more than friends. He's dewy-eyed when he's around you. All those feelings he had for you in his youth are still there. It's obvious to anyone. Put the poor man out of his misery and go on a proper date with him."

"I don't want to. I've only just got divorced. I don't want to get involved with another man."

"Even if he's as handsome as our local police officer?" Peggy asked.

"Yes," I said firmly. "We're friends, and that's it. I'll tell him about the murder thing and Erin's rings when we get home."

Peggy and Erin shared another look, but I turned my back on them and began to tidy up the kitchen. My thoughts went to Seb for a moment. Yes, I did love him when we were young. We grew up together and dated for a while. But that was years ago. We got on well now, and he occasionally came round to my house for a coffee and a chat. But that was all, and that suited me just fine.

When the kitchen and café areas were clean, I said to Erin, "Are you okay to drive home?"

"Of course. Why wouldn't I be?"

"I thought you might still be upset about your rings."

"I am, but you're going to deal with it now." She gave me a swift hug. "I know you'll find them. You're amazing. My favourite sister."

"I'm your only sister. Shall I drive behind you to make sure you get home okay?"

"No. There's no need. But I'll text you when I get home."

"Make sure you do. I'll walk you to your car."

She let out an exasperated sigh. "Karis, it's only parked outside the back door. You have to stop fussing so much."

"I can't help it." Despite her protests, I did follow her to the car. And I watched her drive away.

When I returned to the café, I found Peggy frowning at her phone. She said, "I can't see a thing on this screen. It's too little. I've made the words as big as I can, but they still look fuzzy. There must be something wrong with it."

"What are you looking at?"

"My emails. Someone's sent me an email about tonight's event. I want to know who it is." She gave me the phone. "Here, you look."

I did so. "It's from Lyla Gibson-Smith. Ooo, she's got a fancy name, hasn't she? She says thank you for the event." I read a bit more. "Oh, she says you should be more selective about who attends any future ones."

"Does she? Why? Who is she having a go at?"

I gave the phone back to Peggy. "She doesn't say, but I'm guessing it's Maisie. You should have seen how she looked at her earlier."

"How?"

I said truthfully, "Like she could murder her."

We looked at each other in silence.

Then Peggy said, "Let's get home as quickly as possible. I need to get on my computer. I want to make sure everyone's still alive, especially Maisie. I'm going to phone Anita at the shop too. I didn't like how you had a funny feeling when you met her."

"Why don't you let Seb deal with everything? He's more than capable."

"I know he is, but by the time he gets round to talking to everyone, it could be too late. Karis, we know there's going to be a murder. We have to do what we can to stop it." She rushed towards the door. "Come on. We've got no time to lose."

Chapter 6

I was on tenterhooks all the next day. I had phoned Seb as soon as I'd got home. He'd been very understanding. He's known about my psychic abilities since we were children, and he didn't doubt my vision for a second. There had been a time at school when things went wrong between us, but that was in the past now. He said he'd call on the people who'd been at the event and ask them about the missing rings. He assured me he'd be diplomatic.

That was last night, and I hadn't heard a word from him since. I'd kept myself busy all day with work at the café, and then I'd come home and caught up on my paperwork. Peggy had texted me constantly to see what Seb had discovered, and Erin had sent me questioning looks all day. I kept giving them the same answer: No, I hadn't heard from Seb yet.

Robbie had noticed Erin's missing rings as soon as she'd returned home the previous night, and even though Erin had been prepared to keep the truth from him, one look at his kind face and the truth had come out. Just as I'd known he would, Robbie had been understanding and sympathetic. He'd told Erin to leave everything to Seb. I suspected Robbie would make his own discreet enquiries.

It was getting on for eight o'clock when Seb finally appeared at my door.

"Sorry to call so late," he said. The solemn look on his face caused my heart to miss a beat.

"It's not late. Come in." I opened the door wider and he stepped inside. I didn't close the door immediately. I was expecting another visitor. Sure enough, within five seconds, Peggy was rushing out of her front door and into my house. As well as sharing most aspects of our lives, we lived in either side of a semi-detached house.

"I'm here!" Peggy announced to Seb in the hallway. "I saw your car just now. About time too! We've been waiting for news all day. Don't just stand there. Sit down and tell us everything." She headed into the living room.

Seb looked at me. "She's like a force of nature." His look softened. "How are you?"

"Worried," I admitted. "You've got bad news for us. I can tell."

He laid a hand on my shoulder. "I'm afraid so."

Peggy popped her head around the door. "Oi! Get your hands off Karis. Hurry up and get in here."

Seb gave me a small smile before joining Peggy in the living room. He sat in the armchair next to the window. I joined Peggy on the sofa and waited for him to begin.

He said, "Following your phone call, Karis, I contacted those people who'd attended your event and informed them I wanted to speak to them about a police matter."

Peggy said, "Don't be so formal. Just tell us what happened."

"I'm getting to that," Seb said with just the slightest hint of impatience. "I did visit most of the people on the list, who confirmed they didn't see anyone going into the kitchen. There was one person who couldn't see me until late afternoon. Mrs Lyla Gibson-Smith." He paused for just a fraction of a second, and I knew what he was going to say. "When I called on Mrs Gibson-Smith at her home, she was dead."

Peggy gasped. "Lyla? Are you sure?"

"I am."

"Well, I am surprised," Peggy said. "Of all the people I thought might die, I didn't think it would be her."

"Why?" Seb asked.

"She lives by her own rules and considers herself above everyone, even Death." She shook her head slowly. "But when Death comes knocking at your door, you've got to let him in. Is that what happened? Did someone come knocking at her door? Give us the full details. Don't leave anything out."

I said to her, "Seb might not be able to tell us everything. This is a murder investigation now." I looked at him. "Am I right? Do you suspect murder?"

"We do. I can't tell you much at this point, but there were no signs of forced entry. Her front door was unlocked."

"So, she knew the killer," Peggy surmised. "She must have let them in. How did she die? Can you tell us that?"

"I can show you how she died." He took his phone out. "I knew I'd be talking to you both about Mrs Gibson-Smith's death, so I took a few photos."

Peggy recoiled and sat further back on the sofa. "I don't want to see a dead body, thank you very much. What do you take me for?"

He moved over to us and knelt in front of me. "These are not photos of the deceased, but rather, what killed her. Karis, look at this. Do you recognise it?"

I looked at the image. I broke out in goosebumps. "I do. That's the same cross stitch pattern I was working on." I swallowed. "Where did you find that?"

"It was on the deceased's lap. She'd been working on it shortly before she died. I won't go into details about how she looked, but I suspect she was poisoned. And the poison could have come from the cross stitch itself, either the thread or the material. I don't know much about cross stitch, but Mum does them now and again. And when she threads the needle, she always licks the end of the thread." He hesitated. "Like I said, I won't go into details about the deceased. I've sent the material and thread off for urgent testing."

"Wait." Peggy held her hand up. "Are you saying my cross stitch killed Lyla?"

"Your cross stitch?" Seb asked. "Did you give it to the deceased?"

"Yes, and stop calling her the deceased. I gave a welcome pack to all my guests last night. I put the same kit in all of them." She blanched. "Oh no, does this mean everyone else is in danger?"

Seb straightened up. "They could be. Peggy, I need to know where you got those kits from. I'll contact everyone immediately by phone. We don't want any more deaths."

"I don't understand," Peggy said quietly. "How can this be happening? Is it something I've done? Have I killed Lyla?"

"Where did you get those kits from?" Seb asked.

"Online. From a company I've used before." Her eyes glistened. "I killed Lyla. I gave her a poisoned kit."

I put my hand on her arm. "You didn't kill her. You gave me the same kit, and Erin too. We're still alive. Someone must have done something to Lyla's kit. Seb will find out what."

"I will," Seb confirmed. "But to be on the safe side, I'll collect the others which you've given out. If you've got any spares, I'll take those too. Can I have yours, Karis?"

"Of course. I've got it in the drawer over there." I stood up. "Can I look at that photo again, please? Something doesn't seem right."

Seb showed me the photo of the half-finished project. I told Peggy to look.

She did so and tapped Seb's phone. "That's not the thread I put in the kit. It's a much darker red. Karis, does it look a darker red to you?"

"It does." I collected the fabric and thread and showed it to Seb.

He frowned as he looked at the thread. "This red is a much lighter shade. It could mean Lyla's thread was replaced with a poisoned one. Peggy, how well did you know Lyla?"

"Well enough. Are you going to ask me next if she had any enemies?"

"Well?"

"She did. Plenty of them. She upset everyone she spoke to." Peggy gave me a direct look. "You'd better tell Seb about your vision with Maisie and Lyla."

"She told me last night," Seb told Peggy.

"Oh? On the phone or in person?"

"On the phone." Seb gave us a serious look. "I'm only going to say this once. Leave this investigation to me. Okay? Peggy, okay?"

Her look was full of innocence. "I would never interfere in a police investigation. You have a low opinion of me, DCI Parker."

"I have a realistic opinion of you. I'll see myself out. Karis, I haven't forgotten about Erin's rings, but that will have to wait for a while."

"Of course. She'll understand. If there's anything I can help you with, let me know."

His look softened once more as he looked at me. "Be sensible. Be safe." He gave me a goodbye nod before leaving the house.

When he'd gone, Peggy said, "Right, who should we question first?"

Chapter 7

"You heard what Seb said last night," I told Peggy yet again the next morning as we drove along. "He told us not to interfere."

"You keep telling me that, and I keep telling you that we're not interfering. We are merely going to Hart's Haberdashery to give Anita those unsold kits. That's all. There's no harm in that, is there?"

I knew better than to argue with her. She had an answer for everything. "So, we're going to Anita's shop solely to give her the kits. Then we'll leave. Is that right?"

"We can't just throw them at her and run out of the shop without having a little chat. That wouldn't be polite. We could stay for a few minutes, just to see how she is and how her mum's doing." She rested her hands on her lap and looked out of the window, avoiding my knowing gaze as she did so.

"Don't mention Lyla," I said. "She might not know about her yet."

Still looking out of the window, Peggy said, "If the subject of Lyla comes up, then it would be impolite not to join in."

"You could try."

She smiled. "We'll see."

A few minutes later, we pulled up outside Hart's Haberdashery. The shop had been here for as long as I could remember, but I'd never been inside.

Peggy got out of the car and waited for me on the pavement. With joy in her eyes, she said, "We're about to enter a piece of heaven. Pure heaven." She took a reverent step forward as if she were about to enter a church. I couldn't see what the fuss was about.

Until I stepped inside the shop.

It was like walking back in history. Wooden shelves adorned the walls, each stuffed full with a mixture of materials: balls of wool, rolls of material, boxes of buttons, and layers of threads. The variety of colours was overwhelming and it looked like a hundred rainbows were having a sleep on the shelves. Wired displays stood proudly at the end of the shelves holding zips, needles, hooks and even more threads. There were other items on display too, but I had no idea what they were.

Peggy inhaled deeply. "Can you smell that, Karis? It's creative magic just waiting for us. The smell of wool, fabric and endless possibilities. The aroma of dreams. We can make whatever we want in here. I could live in this shop. I'd be happy to die here too. You could stick my coffin on the highest shelf and that would be totally fine by me."

"I don't think it would be fine for the customers." My eyes were drawn to some framed cross stitch pictures on the walls. "What are those? Are they for sale?"

"I think so. They've been there a while. No one seems to like the travel-poster style anymore."

"I like them." I couldn't take my eyes off the images of far-away places.

Peggy tapped me on the arm. "What do you mean by that? You like them like a normal person would? Or are you drawn to them for psychic reasons?"

I shrugged. "I think I just like them. I'm not getting a strange feeling about them."

We walked further into the shop and past more displays of unfamiliar, at least to me, objects. At the end of the shop was a long wooden counter. Behind it were even more shelves holding tubs of buttons. Just how many buttons did a person need?

To the side of the counter were a couple of round tables set with chairs. Pattern books had been laid neatly on the tables. Behind the tables was an area where customers could help themselves to tea and coffee.

Peggy said, "I've spent a few hours sitting at those tables. I've held a few informal classes there too. Well, not so much classes, more like giving a helping hand to folk who need it but were too shy to ask for help. You know me, I don't like to interfere in people's lives."

I thought it best not to add a comment.

Anita came through a door behind the counter. She broke into a smile. "I thought I heard voices. Peggy, Karis, hello. It's good to see you. How are you both?"

"Fine, just fine. How's your mum?" Peggy asked.

"She's doing well. She's having a sleep."

Peggy put a bag on the table, "Like I said in that email to you, I sold most of your kits the other night. There's only a handful that didn't sell. I've put your takings in an envelope."

"Thanks, Peggy. It's so kind of you to do that. Let me give you something for your trouble."

Peggy held her hands up. "Absolutely not. After how you helped me with that photo project, it's me who should be paying you. Erin was over the moon with it, wasn't she?" She looked my way.

I nodded. "She loved it. She's already put it up in her living room. Robbie, her husband, loves it too. I told everyone about your special offer."

Anita clasped her hands together. "I'm so pleased. Do you know, I've already had someone come in about that. She wants me to make some patterns from her photos. Have you got time for a tea or coffee? You could tell me all about the craft evening."

"As much as I'd love to, we'd better not," Peggy said. "If I stay any longer, I'm going to end up buying things I don't need."

Anita held up a finger. "Don't need, but want. Am I right?"

Peggy laughed. "That's true. My spare bedroom is already full of enough projects to keep me going for the next fifty years. If I live that long." Her smile wavered, and I knew she was thinking about Lyla.

I quickly said, "Anita, I really like those travel-posters pictures on the wall. Are they for sale?"

"You want to buy them?" There was surprise in her voice. "Nobody has ever shown any interest in them before."

"Who made them?" I asked. "You?"

"No, it was one of my regulars. You might know her, Peggy. Lyla Gibson-Smith. I think she's part of your online group, isn't she?"

Peggy calmly replied, "Yes, she is. She made them?"

"She did." Anita lowered her voice even though there was no one else in the shop. "She insisted I put them up for sale. I do that now and again for some people who don't have room in their homes for their completed pictures. I tell them there's no guarantee I'll sell them, but they're okay with that. But it was different with Lyla. She wanted them on display so customers would know where she'd been on her travels. Isn't that a strange thing to do?"

"It is," I agreed. Peggy's lips were pressed tightly together as if she was forcing her words to stay inside her mouth. "How long have they been on the walls?"

"A few years, I think. Maybe more. She wanted me to put her name underneath them, along with details of the hotels she'd stayed in. I didn't like the idea of that, so I firmly told her no. She didn't take that well. I don't think people say no to her often. Her friend didn't like it either." She frowned. "What's her name? That small woman with the brown hair? Peggy, do you know who I mean? I think she went to school with Lyla."

"Kim Webb?" Peggy asked tightly. It was clear she was fighting with her conscience, wanting to tell Anita about Lyla's death but worried what Seb would say if she did.

"That's it!" Anita said. "I'm surprised they're such good friends, considering–" She abruptly stopped talking. "No, I mustn't gossip."

"A little gossip never hurt anyone," Peggy told her. "Go on; you can tell us."

Anita considered the matter for a few moments. "I suppose it is common knowledge. Kim and Lyla were friends all through school, but that changed when Kim got engaged to a local chap. I can't recall his name, but he came from a rich family. She was all set to marry him, but then he called the engagement off and two months later he eloped with Lyla."

"No! That's awful," I said. "Why are they still friends?"

Anita shrugged. "Who knows? Kim and Lyla didn't fall out for long. The husband died a while back, leaving Lyla a wealthy woman. That's why she goes on so many holidays. Kim goes with her, I think. Are you sure you still like those pictures, Karis? After what you know about Lyla?"

"I think so." I gave her an uncertain smile. "I'll buy them anyway. I can give them to a charity shop if I change my mind."

"That's good enough for me. I'll get them down now before you do change your mind. You can have them for nothing. Think of them as a thank you gift for selling those kits of mine."

She rushed out from the counter and over to the pictures at an impressive speed. The pictures were off the walls, wrapped up and placed in my hands within five minutes.

Anita returned to her position behind the counter and said, "It's strange that we're talking about Lyla because she's the one who brought those photos in to me yesterday. She wants them turned into patterns."

"She came in here?" Peggy stiffened. "I don't suppose you can show us the photos? Just out of curiosity on my part."

I shot Peggy a warning look, but she chose to ignore it.

"Of course I can." Anita pulled a folder out from under the counter. She put it on the counter and took out a handful of photographs. She fanned them out. "I'm not sure whether Lyla does want me to make her a pattern, or whether she wanted to show off about all the cruises she's been on. As you can see, these are all holiday pictures."

Peggy and I stared at the photos. One caught my eye. Or rather, it was someone in the background who had caught my eye. I cast a quick look at Peggy. She looked at me and gave me the slightest of nods. She'd seen the same person.

Before we could take a closer look, a shadow fell over us.

Peggy and I slowly turned around to face Seb.

His face was devoid of emotion. I saw a plastic bag in his hand. Dark red thread was inside. The thread which had belonged to Lyla?

"DCI Parker!" Peggy announced far too loudly. "Fancy seeing you here. Buying some supplies for your mum, are you? Oh, you don't have to answer that of course! You could be here on police business. Not that I'm an expert on what you police do. No, not me. Come on, Karis. We'd better be getting on. Bye Anita! Love to your mum."

Seb's face was still expressionless as we moved around him. No doubt, we would have a lot of explaining to do later.

As if we weren't in enough trouble already, Peggy yanked on his sleeve, pulled him closer and hissed, "Take a good look at those photos on the counter!"

His response was to raise one eyebrow.

With that, Peggy and I left the shop, almost at a run.

Chapter 8

I couldn't drive away fast enough from Hart's Haberdashery. I was aware Seb could be standing at the window shooting us annoyed looks. I said to Peggy, "We're in trouble now. Seb told us to keep out of his investigation. And look where he finds us."

"We weren't interfering in his investigation. We were merely paying a visit to a friend of mine on a business matter. We didn't know Seb was going to be there. What was he doing there anyway? I bet he was going to ask Anita about that red thread. Did you see the bag in his hand? I wonder if Lyla bought it from Anita's shop?" She held her hand up. "Not that it's any of my business. I'm leaving Seb to get on with his work. I'm keeping right out of it."

I kept my eyes on the road and said, "But we did talk about Lyla with Anita. And we saw those photographs she'd brought in."

"It was Anita who brought the subject of Lyla up, wasn't it? We didn't encourage her to do so. Anyway, let Seb think what he wants. But while we're on the subject, did you see who was in those photos? The person in the uniform behind Lyla?"

I nodded. "It was Maisie. She must have been working on that cruise ship. It was a cruise ship, wasn't it? Going by the background, it looked like one to me."

"Me too. Did you see how Lyla was sitting? It was at an awkward angle as if she was trying to get Maisie in the photograph. And did you see the smug look on her face as if she was taking pleasure in Maisie waiting hand and foot on passengers like herself?"

"I did notice that."

Peggy said, "I wonder how many times they'd come across each other on those ships. It's all very interesting, don't you think? Considering that vision you had about them at school, and how they didn't let on they knew each other the other night. When all the time, it's obvious they did."

I shot her a quick look before asking, "Do you think Maisie killed Lyla? And it's got something to do with her past?"

"Who knows? That's for Seb to find out." She stopped talking for about two seconds. "Or we could ask around and see what we can find out about Maisie."

"No," I told her firmly. "Let's just leave everything to the police."

She mumbled something but I didn't catch her words.

A noise came from my bag on the back seat. I said, "That's my phone. Would you mind answering it for me? Thanks."

Peggy reached for my bag and retrieved my phone. "If it's Seb, I'm going to pretend to be you. I'll use all my womanly wiles on him and get some information out of him."

"I haven't got any womanly wiles. If it's Seb, tell him I'll phone him back."

Peggy looked at the screen. "It's Erin. Shall I answer it?"

My hands tightened on the steering wheel. "Yes! I hope she's okay. I hope she hasn't gone into early labour."

"You worry too much about that girl." Peggy answered the phone and immediately said, "Erin! Are you okay? Have you gone into premature labour? Are you at the hospital?" She listened to Erin's reply and then said, "She's there at the café right now? And she wants to see us?" A pause. "Okay. We'll be there soon. You take care. Bye for now." She put the phone on her lap.

"Well?" I asked. "Who's waiting for us at the café?"

"Now, before you start giving me a lecture, I didn't ask her to meet us. And if she wants to talk to us, then we'll have to listen to what she wants to tell us. It would be very rude if we didn't turn up."

"Who are you talking about?"

"Maisie Abbot. She's at the cafe and asked Erin to get in touch with us. I wonder what she wants to talk about? It could be something or nothing. We won't know until we get there."

I was in two minds. Should I get in touch with Seb and ask him if it was alright to talk to Maisie? But there again, like Peggy said, we didn't know what she wanted to talk about.

I changed direction and headed towards the café. I said, "I wonder if she knows about Lyla's death yet? Seb must have been in touch with her about getting those cross stitch kits back."

"Ah," Peggy held a finger up. "I didn't give one to Maisie because she came in late. So, maybe he hasn't spoken to her yet. But he might have talked to her about Erin's missing rings. We don't know, do we? He should have told us who he's spoken to, and what he said."

"He doesn't have to tell us anything." I felt Peggy's eyes on me and glanced her way. "Why are you looking at me like that?"

"You defend Seb a lot. You're quite protective of him."

I shrugged. "I'd be like that with any police officer."

"Of course you would. When we talk to Maisie, keep in mind that she might be a suspect. And you know who else is a suspect? Lyla's best friend. There's something about Kim Webb I just don't like. I can't imagine why she would be friends with Lyla considering how Lyla got her hooks into Kim's boyfriend. It all seems very weird to me, don't you think?"

I answered, "I'm trying not to think about Lyla's murder at all."

A little chuckle came from Peggy. "Karis, you're such a liar. You're just as eager as me to find out what happened to her."

I didn't bother to argue because Peggy was right.

A short while later, we were sitting in the upstairs area of the café opposite Maisie. She looked worried and I wondered if she was going to make a confession to us. Despite her being a possible suspect, I couldn't help but give her a warm smile. Perhaps I was being too polite.

She delved into her bag and brought out a couple of wrapped bottles. "This is to say thank you for the event the other night. I wasn't sure I was going to be brave enough to make it, but I'm so glad I made the effort."

Peggy took the wine. "There's no need for this, but thank you anyway. I'm glad you made it too. I loved the cross stitch map you did. You've certainly had lots of adventures on your trips around the world. You never told us what your job is."

"Didn't I? I thought I had. I used to work on cruise ships." She gave us a small smile. "I went all around the world many times and met some wonderful people. I didn't tell you this before, but I grew up in this town. I left to work on the ships when I was eighteen."

"That's very young," I said.

Maisie nodded. "To be honest, I had to get away from my family."

"Oh?" Peggy asked. "Why was that? If you don't mind me asking."

Maisie gave her a wry smile. "I changed my surname when I left town. When I tell you what my original name was, you'll know why I left. It was Scargrange."

Peggy's eyebrows shot up in surprise. "Scargrange? You do surprise me."

I said, "I've never heard that name before."

"Then you're lucky," Maisie answered. "My family has a terrible reputation in this town. They're petty thieves and blackmailers. They've been involved in all sorts of dodgy dealings over the years. I was never like that, but I was tarred with the same brush. No matter how well I behaved, people were always ready to believe the worst of me."

Peggy and I shared a look. I wondered if she was talking about Lyla.

Maisie continued, "Something happened at school, and the finger of blame came towards me once again. I was innocent, but no one believed a Scargrange. I knew I couldn't stay in this town and be blamed for any future crimes my family committed. So, I got a job working on the ships and never looked back. I only returned to town at Mum's request. She wanted me to make amends with my family, but I told her it would be hard to do that when they're all in prison. And they'll be there for the next few years."

Peggy nodded. "I had heard about that. It's your dad and your brothers who are locked up, isn't that right?"

Maisie nodded. "That's right. Poor Mum had to put up with a lot through the years. Even when I left to work on the ships, I kept in touch with her to make sure she was okay. She kept saying she was, but I felt guilty about being so far away from her. When she asked me to come back here urgently last month, I knew something was wrong. And I was right. She died a week after I came back. I'm living in her house at the moment getting everything sorted out. My brothers and Dad didn't even have the decency to go to her funeral, even though they were allowed to. They don't have a shred of decency between them."

Her eyes filled with tears.

Peggy place her hand on Maisie's arm. "I'm sorry to hear about your mum. She had a lot of crosses to bear in her life. Are you going to stay in this town now? Or are you going back to the cruise ships?"

She blinked away her tears. "I was going to stay, but then I saw someone from my past who's made that impossible."

"Are you talking about Lyla Gibson-Smith?" I asked.

She gave me a look of surprise.

I explained. "I saw how she looked at you the other night."

Maisie's small smile was almost imperceptible. "You're very observant." She looked left and right. "I'm glad there's no one here because I've got a confession to make."

Chapter 9

I moved slightly forward on my chair. Peggy did too. We silently waited for Maisie to confess.

She began, "Lyla and I were at school together. Something terrible happened between us. Something I've tried to put behind me." She stopped talking and looked at the table.

"You don't have to talk about it," I said, "not if it's upsetting you."

Peggy interjected, "As upsetting as it is, it sometimes helps to talk about these things."

Maisie lifted her head. "You could be right about that, Peggy. Okay, here goes. When I was at school, my family's reputation followed me through every year. I did my best to ignore the gossip and suspicious looks people gave me. I worked hard at my lessons and kept out of trouble. Everything seemed to be going well. I made lots of friends along the way, apart from Lyla. For some reason, she just didn't like me. I wasn't sure why."

"Maybe it's because you had lots of friends and you worked hard," I suggested. I thought back to my school days and how people had made fun of my psychic abilities.

Maisie continued, "I tried to make friends with her, but she always made fun of me when I did so. Then out of the blue one year, Lyla invited me to her birthday party which she was having at her house. She always made a big deal about her parties and who was invited, and more importantly, who wasn't. It was the first year I'd received an invite, and I wasn't sure whether to go or not. But Lyla spoke to me after class one day and said she wanted to apologise for all the terrible lies she'd told about me. I wasn't even aware she had been spreading lies about me."

Peggy tutted in disgust.

"So, despite my better judgement, I decided to go to Lyla's party. It was wonderful, to begin with. Lyla and her best friend Kim made me feel very welcome. They were at my side at the beginning of the night and kept telling me gossip about the other people who were there. I didn't like to gossip, so I felt uncomfortable. But you know what young girls are like; they want their peers to think well of them. To blend into the crowd and not stand out."

I nodded. I knew that feeling.

Maisie said, "For some reason, Lyla and Kim invited me into Lyla's bedroom to look at the presents her parents had got her. I'd never seen such expensive jewellery before. I remember how eager Lyla was for me to touch a particular gold necklace. It made me feel uneasy. They continued to gossip about other people, and their comments turned really nasty. I knew I couldn't stay there and listen anymore. I made an excuse and went home." Her look hardened, but she didn't say anything.

I asked her, "Did something happen after the party?" Was she going to tell us about the showdown I'd witnessed in my vision?

Maisie nodded. "The very next day, Lyla and Kim confronted me in the hallway at school. It was lunchtime, and there were lots of people walking along the hall. Thinking about it now, I think Lyla wanted an audience. She loudly accused me of stealing her gold necklace from her bedroom the previous night. I denied it. But she said stealing was in my family's nature and I was just like the rest of my family." Maisie's cheeks flushed. "I still feel the shame of it now. I kept saying I didn't do it. But Lyla wouldn't listen, even when I broke down in tears. I don't know why she made up those lies about me. I'd never done anything to her except try to be friends."

I could feel the despair and sadness coming from Maisie. I said gently, "What happened next?"

"My life was ruined. At least, that's what I thought at that young age. People believed all the lies Lyla and Kim told about me. I tried to be brave, but there came a point where I just couldn't take it anymore. Some of my closest friends said they didn't believe what Lyla had told them, but they were never the same with me after that. It didn't help that my brothers were constantly in trouble for local thefts which occurred. My family name was mud, no matter how I behaved. I couldn't wait to leave school. And I couldn't get out of this town fast enough. I worked as many part-time jobs as I could to get money. And then I escaped. But when I came here the other night and saw Lyla and Kim, all those awful memories came back to me."

I said, "Maisie, something similar happened to me at school. People made fun of me for years. But you can't let nasty people from your past affect your life now."

She gave us a smile. "You're absolutely right. I know that. Which is why I'm not going to let Lyla and Kim get to me anymore. When I saw them the other night, my first thought was to leave town immediately. But I've got Mum's things to sort out, and I'm not going to leave that to anyone else. Mum deserved better."

It was obvious Maisie didn't know about Lyla's death yet, and I wasn't going to be the one to tell her.

Peggy said cautiously, "We've just come from Anita's shop and she showed us some photos which Lyla had given her. She wanted them to be made into cross stitch patterns, like the one I did for Erin. There was a picture of Lyla on one of her cruises. You were in the background. Did you often come across Lyla when she was working?"

Maisie stared at Peggy for a moment. Then her shoulders dropped and she looked as if she was going to say something. But someone clearing their throat behind us stopped her.

We looked towards the stairs. A man was standing there.

Peggy muttered, "Not him again. Karis, let's get out of here. Don't forget your wine."

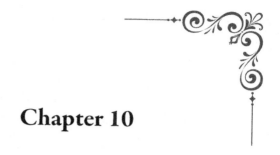

Chapter 10

I was all for leaving the café, jumping in my car and driving away from DCI Parker as quickly as I could. But Erin had other ideas.

She was waiting for us at the bottom of the stairs. She asked, "Have you got time for a cup of tea and some cake? I'm trying out a new cake recipe and I could do with your opinion." Her hand rested on her round stomach. How was I supposed to say no to her?

I cast a glance upwards, half expecting Seb to be watching us. He wasn't, so I said, "Okay. We can stay a while."

Erin gave me a narrow-eyed look. "Why are you looking so shifty? Is it something to do with Seb? Shouldn't I have told him where you were? He came here to tell me he hasn't located my rings yet. I told him you were upstairs, and he was up there in a flash. And the next minute, you two come running down looking guilty. What's going on?"

I took her gently by the elbow and steered her away from the stairs, aware Seb could be listening. In a low voice, I said, "Do you know about Lyla?"

"Lyla? The loud woman who was here at the cross stitch evening?" Her eyes widened. In a hushed voice she said, "Has she...you know?" She looked at the surrounding customers, not wanting to alert them.

I gave her a brief nod. "Yes. It happened yesterday."

Peggy added, "Seb told us not to interfere in his investigation, which we aren't doing. Maisie came here of her own accord to talk to us. That's right, isn't it Erin? And that's what you'll tell that policeman if he asks. You tell him exactly what Maisie said to you."

"Why would he be talking to Maisie?" She absentmindedly rubbed her stomach. "Is she a suspect?"

"We don't know. But we do know Lyla made her life a misery at school." I took Erin over to a quiet corner table and sat her down.

She said, "Tell me more. How did Lyla, you know...move on?"

I said quietly, "Seb seems to think poison was involved. We haven't got all the details."

"Poison? How? In a drink? Something she ate?"

I noticed a few customers turning their heads slightly as if listening to our words.

I shot Erin a warning look and said, "I'll tell you later. Where's this new cake of yours? Is it in the kitchen? I'll get it."

Erin stood up. "You stay right where you are. I'm more than capable of walking into the kitchen myself. Won't be a minute. Don't go anywhere."

When she'd gone, Peggy whispered, "I think Seb has put a tracking device on us. How did he know where to find us?"

"According to Erin, he didn't know we'd be here."

We both glanced at the ceiling.

Peggy said, "Why's he still up there? He must be talking to Maisie. What about? Does he think she's a suspect too?"

"Maybe. He'll have done background checks on everyone. Isn't that how it works?"

"I've no idea. He doesn't tell us anything. If she is a suspect, I wouldn't blame her. Not that murder is the answer, ever. But I can imagine how annoyed and upset Maisie must have been when she came in here and saw her nemesis. As if dealing with her mum's death wasn't bad enough."

I said, "Do you believe what Maisie told us about that gold necklace? The scene does match up with what I saw in my vision."

"I do believe her. But she could be lying to us about what really happened. What if she did steal that necklace?" Her voice lowered a fraction. "If Maisie is a thief, she could have stolen Erin's rings too."

"You could be right. I know Kim went missing at one point, but so did Maisie when she went to get Erin a glass of water." I gave Peggy an urgent shush and indicated my head towards the stairs. I hissed, "Maisie's coming down the steps now. She looks as if she's been crying."

Maisie came over to us. Her eyes were red-rimmed. "I've just heard about Lyla. Isn't it awful? I know I didn't like her, but I would never wish her harm. This is such a shock." She let out a sigh. "DCI Parker would like to talk to you both. He's still upstairs." She shook her head. "I just can't take this in. I really can't." She gave us a weak smile before leaving the café.

Erin came over with the cake and tea. She raised her eyebrows in question as the door closed behind Maisie. Not wanting to discuss the murder with eager ears around us, I said quietly, "I'll phone you later and tell you everything. Seb wants a word with us."

"You're in trouble now," Erin said with a smile. "You'll have to use your womanly wiles on him."

Peggy stood up. "That's what I told her."

"And I told you I haven't got any womanly wiles."

Peggy let out a noise which sounded more like a cackle than a laugh. She picked her tea and cake up. She said, "Perhaps I'll have to use my womanly wiles instead. I've got plenty. Thanks for this, Erin. The cake looks delicious."

We took our cake and tea upstairs and found Seb sitting at the table with a stern look on his face. I wasn't sure about my womanly wiles, but I had cake. I sat down and passed it to him. "Cake? It's a new recipe Erin's trying."

"No, thank you," he said tersely, and pushed the cake back to me. "I don't know where to begin with you two. But I'm not surprised. You just can't help yourselves, can you?"

Peggy sat down and explained, "Maisie wanted to talk to us about a personal matter. It's not our fault that you keep turning up and catch us talking to persons of interest. Is Maisie a person of interest?"

"I'm not going to tell you that," Seb replied. "But you are getting in my way a lot today. You can't deny that."

"Now, just a minute!" Peggy wagged a finger at him.

Seb broke into a smile. "I know why you were here, and why you were at the haberdashery. But it's nice to see you squirm, Mrs Marshall."

She gave him a disgruntled look. "I was going to buy you a cup of tea, but I won't now. Seeing as you're here, can you tell us any more about your precious investigation? Have you found out exactly how Lyla died yet?"

"You know full well I can't give you any details. But I can tell you that poison was definitely the cause of death. It was on the thread and the material. The kits from your welcome packs have been checked, and they're free from poison. But that's all I'm telling you."

Peggy wasn't ready to let the matter drop. "Have you spoken to Maisie about those photographs in Anita's shop?"

Seb replied, "That's none of your business. But I suspect you've already asked Maisie about them."

Peggy relented. "I did, but you turned up before she could answer me. Did you know Lyla's friend, Kim Webb, was due to marry someone years ago, but he ended up marrying Lyla instead?"

"I am aware of Lyla's background." Seb looked at me and his expression softened somewhat. "Karis, Maisie told me about the supposed theft which took place when she was at school. She told me about the confrontation Lyla had with her. She confirmed she'd told you and Peggy the same thing. Does it match the vision you had?"

"It does. I hate to ask this, but is Maisie a suspect?"

"I really can't say, but I'm sure you've already considered her as one. I can tell you that Lyla upset many people over the last few months for one reason and another, and I've got plenty of people to question." He got to his feet. "I don't know whether I should bother saying this again to you both, but please, keep away from anyone associated with Lyla. Someone murdered her, and if they know you're asking questions, they could try to silence you. And I would hate anything to happen to you." He smiled at Peggy. "And I'm talking about both of you."

Peggy returned his smile. "I know you are."

Seb added, "If you do hear anything that might help me, I'd appreciate it if you could contact me immediately." He gave us a swift smile before leaving us.

Peggy shook her head at his departure. "I wish he'd make his mind up. Either he wants us to completely leave his investigation alone, or he wants us to help him."

"I don't think he actually wants us to help him," I attempted to argue, "but we can't help getting involved sometimes, can we?"

"We can't. Let's forget about Lyla for a bit. This cake looks delicious." She picked up her fork and dug it into the cake.

I tucked into mine. But not for long.

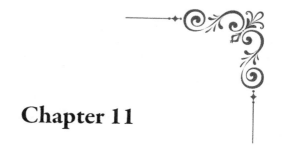

Chapter 11

As I ate the cake, I felt a tickle on my left hand. I gave my hand a quick scratch.

Peggy was saying something about the next craft evening she was planning, but I wasn't paying her much attention. My mind kept wandering to Lyla Gibson-Smith.

The itch on my hand intensified. I scratched it again.

Someone must have called on Lyla on the afternoon she died. Someone she knew. How did they get poison on the thread and the fabric? Did they bring some poisoned thread with them?

My hand was itching like crazy now, but the tickle was centred on my ring finger. I gave it a firm rub.

Peggy put her fork down and said, "What's wrong with you? Are you allergic to something?"

I frowned. "No, it's my finger. It feels really weird as if there's something there. But obviously, there isn't. It's probably nothing."

She looked at my finger. "It's gone red. Why don't you nip to the bathroom and give your hands a wash? Something could be irritating you."

I stood up and headed towards the bathroom, but as I walked past the windows, someone outside on the street caught my attention. "Peggy, come here. Quickly!"

She rushed over to my side and looked out of the window with me. "Is that Kim Webb rushing down the street?"

"Yes. She's almost running." I winced. My finger began to throb with pain now. "I think my itchy finger has something to do with Kim Webb. She might be the thief."

Peggy moved closer to the window so that her face was almost touching it. "I think you could be right. Look how quickly she's walking. The swift walk of a guilty person. Come on; we need to follow her."

I was about to argue that we should keep well away from Kim, but the pain in my finger was becoming more intense by the second. I knew for certain now it had something to do with Kim.

We quickly left the café with a brief wave at Erin and then headed along the street in the direction Kim had gone. We couldn't see her now, but as we rushed past a jewellers' window, the hair on the back of my neck lifted and I came to a sudden stop. I grabbed Peggy's arm and said urgently, "We have to go inside this shop right now. I can't explain why, but we have to."

Peggy gave me a brisk nod in reply.

We went inside and over to the man behind the counter. When he noticed our approach, he grabbed something off the counter and put it somewhere underneath.

My ring finger felt like it was on fire now, and it was taking all my willpower not to cry with pain.

Peggy noticed my distress and said, "Leave the talking to me."

The man gave us a wide smile and asked, "What can I help you with?"

Peggy asked, "Has a woman with dark hair been in here just now?"

"Nope." His smile was still wide.

"You're lying," Peggy said whilst giving him an intense stare. "She came in here and sold some rings to you. Admit it."

His smile faltered slightly. "I don't recall that happening."

Peggy slapped her hand on the counter. "Stop lying. That woman was Kim Webb. You know it was."

"Kim who? Who's that then? And who are you coming here demanding answers from me?"

Peggy wagged a finger at him. "Stop messing about now, Craig Henderson. I've known you since you were a baby, and you know full well who I am. And what's more, I think you know who Kim Webb is. She came in here with a couple of rings. I want the truth, nothing but the truth. Or else I'll be having strong words with your mum."

Craig pulled at the collar of his shirt. "I don't know what you're talking about."

"Oh yes, you do," Peggy said darkly. "Those rings were stolen from someone I care a good deal about. We have a trusted contact in the police department. It would give me great pleasure to let him know you deal with stolen items. Shall I phone him? Or do you want to come clean?" She gave him one of her hard looks and he seemed to wilt.

If I was on the other end of Peggy's stare, I think I'd be wilting too.

"Okay," Craig relented. "It was Kim Webb who brought two rings in for me. She said she didn't need them anymore and I could have them at a cheap price. That's all I know."

I asked, "Can I have a look at the rings? I think they belong to my sister."

He reluctantly reached for something under the counter and then put them in front of us.

I looked at them but didn't pick them up. The itch on my finger lessened considerably. "Those are Erin's rings. They were stolen recently." I said to Peggy, "I really want to take these back to Erin, but we should let Seb know about this."

"I agree," she said. "Craig, we're going to phone the police and let them know about this. It's important you talk to them and confirm who brought them in and what she said."

He shook his head. "I didn't know they were stolen. Take them back if they belong to your sister. I don't want anything to do with them."

Peggy said to him, "It's too late for that now. You should have thought of that when Kim came in here with guilt written all over her face."

"She looked normal to me. In fact, she looked a bit happier than she normally does. And I was surprised to see her on her own. She's usually with that Lyla when I've seen her around town." He leaned on the counter as if settling in for a good gossip. "I knew them at school. I never knew why they were friends. Total opposites they are. Have they fallen out? I hope so. I never liked Lyla. She had a nasty streak running through her. Has she got something to do with these stolen rings?"

Peggy said indignantly, "I don't indulge in idle gossip. We're going to phone the police in a minute or two. When they come here, you'd better give them the full details because I'll know if you don't."

Craig straightened up and muttered, "Okay."

I reluctantly left the rings with Craig and walked out of the shop with Peggy. Once outside, I phoned Seb but he didn't answer. I left him a message about the rings and explained how my itchy finger had led us to it. I didn't go into details about Peggy and me running after Kim Webb. He didn't need to know everything.

Peggy looked deep in thought and I asked her what she was thinking about.

"It's those rings," she said. "I think Kim was going to plant them on Maisie and accuse her of stealing them. But why didn't she do that the other night when everyone was at the café? She must have had the opportunity to do so. And if that was the plan, did Lyla tell her to do it?"

I followed Peggy's train of thought. "Maybe. Perhaps Kim didn't want to. It's one thing doing that at school, but another when you're an adult." I sighed. "What if Lyla had something over Kim which made Kim do her bidding? It could have been the last straw for Kim and she decided to do away with Lyla."

"I was thinking that too. Craig said Kim looked happy when she came in. She must know about Lyla's death by now. Surely?"

We stood there mulling the matter over, but didn't know what to say.

I put my phone away and said, "Let's leave everything to the police. I've had enough of talking about murder for one day."

"Me too," Peggy agreed. "How's your finger?"

"Much better, thanks." I looked at my hand and hoped I wouldn't be having any more psychic episodes today.

Chapter 12

I spent the rest of the day studiously not discussing the murder investigation, but it was hard to do as I was working at the café with my sister. Erin kept trying to get me to to discuss the case, but I refused to do so, and declared it was in the hands of the police. She didn't like my answer, but there was nothing I could do about that. I didn't have to discuss the situation with Peggy because she was busy with her hospital visits. Not only did she keep herself busy with café-related events and her blog, she made time to visit friends in the hospital. I really didn't know where she got her energy from.

I purposely kept myself busy all day so that I'd be exhausted when I got home. I had a nagging feeling that I should be finding out more about Lyla and her untimely death. It felt like some invisible being was tapping me on the shoulder and saying, "I haven't finished with you yet." I was hoping that if I kept working, I'd be too tired to think straight soon.

As I pulled my car into the driveway later that day, I noticed Peggy tapping on her living room window. I got out of my car and waved to her. She beckoned me over. Had something else happened?

She opened the door to me. "You look all done in. Do you want to stay for dinner? I've made a chicken and leek pie, and I've got some roast potatoes and vegetables to go with it. I thought we could do with a comforting meal after today's events. What do you say?"

"That sounds wonderful. Just what I need. Thank you." I nodded in the direction of my car. "I'll just put those pictures Anita gave me in my house. I don't want to forget about them."

"Oh! I already had forgotten about them." Peggy gave me a searching look. "Have you had any funny feelings about them? Any visions?"

"No. Not yet anyway. I didn't get any funny feelings in Anita's shop either. I just like the look of them, that's all."

"If you say so."

I went to the boot of my car and retrieved the wrapped pictures. I don't know whether it was Peggy's words or whether it was the pictures themselves, but I did get a tingly feeling in my fingers. Instead of taking the pictures into my own house, I took them into Peggy's.

She gave me a knowing look as she closed the front door behind me. She said, "I thought you might have been drawn to them for a reason. Sit yourself down and let's see what happens next."

"I think I'd be better doing this on my own," I told her. "It's not easy having visions if someone's watching me. I hope you understand."

"Of course. No one wants an audience when they're doing this sort of thing. Unless you're one of those charlatans on the stage who get paid to do it. I'll leave you alone then. I'll get the dinner on. Shout out if you need me." She gave me a smile before disappearing into the kitchen.

I sat on the sofa and unwrapped the pictures. I was drawn again to the lovely images of the faraway destinations. How wonderful it must be to travel so easily to these places.

I picked the one of Bali up and placed it squarely on my knee. My hands were tingling even more now as I lightly ran them over the cross stitch pattern. Even though I'd only done a small cross stitch project myself, I admired the needlework. This was a complicated pattern and it must have taken Lyla a long time to do.

I traced my fingers over the beach part of the image and ran my fingers along one of the palm trees. Ouch! I pulled my hand back as a shooting sensation shot through my fingers. It was like a dozen needles had stabbed me. I peered closer at the image and couldn't see anything sticking out.

I carefully repeated the manoeuvre, and yet again felt that stabbing pain when my fingers went over the tree. An urge came over me which I couldn't ignore. A quick look through Peggy's cupboard provided me with what I needed. Part of me was thinking that I shouldn't be doing this at all, but that was overridden by an unstoppable urge to find out why that tree was hurting me. With great concentration, I began to cut the stitches along the tree.

I was so engrossed in my work, that I didn't hear Peggy come into the room. But I certainly heard her scream out in horror. "Karis! What on earth are you doing! You vandal! Stop that!"

I paused in mid-cut and looked her way. "I didn't hear you come in."

She came over to me. "That's obvious. You were too engrossed in your act of vandalism. What's got into you? Look at what you've done to that lovely tree."

I looked back at the picture and moved some of the cut stitches out of the way. "I had to do it. Peggy, look at this. There's something written on the fabric underneath the stitches. I can only make out a few words so far."

She sat next to me and had a closer look. "Well, I never. You're right. It's a bit hard to make out because the thread is only a shade or two darker than the fabric."

I carefully cut a few more stitches. When the bark of the tree had gone, I moved on to the leaves. Peggy silently watched my every move.

A short while later, we were able to read the embroidered words.

Peggy was the first to let out a surprised gasp. "I can't believe it! What awful words to write! And under such a beautiful image too. It's despicable."

I nodded. "It's clear Lyla hated Maisie with a vengeance. Look at all these names she's called her. And how many times she's written that she loathes her."

Peggy pointed to a line of vertical words. "Look at that. Lyla has even written about how she would murder Maisie if she ever got the chance. What vile things to write. And then she asked Anita to put this picture on the wall in full view of everyone. That Lyla must have been chuckling to herself every time someone looked at this picture. What a nasty person she was."

I put the damaged picture to one side. "I haven't checked the other one yet."

I picked up the travel-poster image of Jamaica and began the process of running my hands over it. Again, I got the stabbing sensation which guided me towards the right areas to uncover. The words we found hidden underneath were even worse.

Peggy said quietly, "Lyla must have used a thesaurus to get that many words. And she's certainly been creative with all the ways she wanted to kill Maisie. What had Maisie ever done to Lyla to make her hate her so much?"

"That's a good question. Maybe Maisie had to leave all those years ago because of something terrible she did to Lyla. Perhaps she did steal the necklace after all. She could have been lying to us at the café earlier."

"Perhaps. When Maisie came to our craft evening, Lyla must have been furious at seeing her. What if Lyla threatened to tell everyone what she was really like? And Maisie couldn't have that, so she decided to kill Lyla." She frowned. "I hope I'm wrong about Maisie, though. I like her."

I tapped the picture. "You can't argue with these words. I think there's a lot more to Lyla and Maisie's relationship then Maisie is telling us. And there's one person who could give us some more information, and that's Kim Webb. But we can't go and question her, can we? We'll have to tell Seb about this."

Peggy surprised me by saying, "Of course. We should let him know." She stiffened. "Hang on a moment. What if Kim knows that Maisie killed Lyla? After all, she was friends with Lyla and would know how Lyla truly felt about Maisie. What if Kim is on her way to confront Maisie? Or hurt her? She could be there right now!"

I reached for my phone. "I'll phone Seb."

Peggy shot to her feet. "There's no time. We have to go to Maisie's immediately."

"But we don't know where she lives."

"I do. She's at her mum's house. It's a fifteen-minute drive away. Come on! There could be another murder. We have to do something."

She jumped as a loud knock sounded out.

Her hands went to her chest. "It's the murderer! Hide."

I stood up. "I know that knock. It's Seb."

"What's he doing here? Are we too late? Has there been another murder?" She dashed to the door and opened it. I was right behind her. She shouted at Seb, "Who's dead now?"

Seb frowned at her. "No one. Why are you asking me that? What's going on now? What have you done?"

Peggy sagged against the door frame. "Thank goodness no one else has died. What are you doing here?"

"I wanted to let you know someone has admitted to killing Lyla."

"It's Maisie, isn't it?" Peggy said. "It must be."

"No, it's not Maisie." He paused. "It's Kim Webb. She's made a confession."

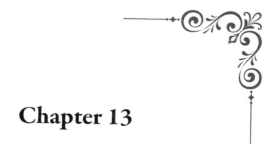

Chapter 13

Seb refused to give us any more information before he turned away and left.

Peggy shook her head as we returned to the living room. "I don't understand. Why would Kim kill Lyla? My money was on Maisie."

"Perhaps Kim had been pushed too far by Lyla. Seb didn't tell us anything about Erin's rings or why Kim had stolen them. It might have something to do with her confession."

Peggy frowned. "I hate getting half a story. Oh well, I'm sure we'll get the full facts at some point." She gave me a considered look. "But Kim saying she murdered Lyla doesn't feel right to me. How about you?"

"I feel the same. I wonder if she's covering up for someone?"

"Maisie?"

I shrugged. "I really don't know."

Her attention went to the damaged cross stitch pictures. "You never got the chance to show these to Seb. I don't suppose it matters now."

"No, I don't suppose it does. I'll tidy them away. And I'll pick up those bits of thread. Sorry, I didn't mean to make such a mess."

"I know you didn't. You can't help yourself when you get in one of your psychic states. I'll get our dinner ready while you do that."

She left the room and I soon heard her moving about in the kitchen.

I took a long look at the words on the pictures. These were important, and I got a feeling I should have told Seb about them. But why were they so important? If Kim had confessed, why did it matter now how much Lyla had hated Maisie Abbot?

A short while later, I was sitting at the kitchen table with Peggy. The food was delicious. Warm and comforting. Just what we both needed.

Peggy chatted about some of the friends whom she'd visited in hospital. She said, "I think I'll go and see them again tomorrow. Some of them looked lonely. I don't think they get many visitors."

"You are kind, Peggy."

"You'd do the same if I was in hospital, wouldn't you?" There was the smallest flicker of doubt in her eyes.

"Of course I would! You're family. Erin would visit you, and so would Robbie. I'm sure Seb would even turn up."

She smiled. "I doubt that. Not unless I'd been up to no good and he wanted to interrogate me. Have you got room for dessert?"

"Always."

We finished eating and our talk turned to other matters. We discussed everything except Lyla's murder. I guessed it was still on Peggy's mind, just as it was still on mine. Something didn't feel right about the whole thing. I felt we were missing something obvious.

It was another hour before we said goodnight to each other. I collected the damaged cross stitch pictures and walked the short distance to my house. Thoughts of Lyla were buzzing around my brain like pesky bees. I wished they would go away.

But they didn't.

I knew I wouldn't be able to sleep for a while, so once inside my home, I settled down on the sofa and attempted to read a book. But I found myself staring into the distance time and time again. I felt like I was waiting for comprehension to dawn on me. If that was the case, it was certainly taking its time.

Around eleven o'clock, there was a soft knock at the front door. I didn't hesitate to open it because I knew who it would be.

Seb gave me a sheepish smile. In a low voice, he said, "Sorry to disturb you. I saw your light was on. Can we talk?" His glance went to Peggy's house as if expecting her to race out of her house and leap over the low fence at any second.

"Come in. You haven't disturbed me. I couldn't sleep. Would you like a hot drink? Or a cold one? Wine?"

He came in and I closed the door behind him. He said, "No, thanks. I am off-duty but I don't want to put you to any trouble."

"You're not. I'm going to have a small glass of wine. It might help me sleep. Are you sure you don't want one?"

"Well, if you're going to twist my arm like that, how can I say no?" He grinned at me and looked like the young man I remembered so well.

I told him to take a seat while I got our drinks. When I returned from the kitchen, I found him staring intently at the ruined pictures. He said, "What's happened here? Who destroyed these pictures?"

"I did. They belonged to Lyla." I handed him the wine. Then I told him about the hidden words and pointed them out on the pictures.

"Wow. Those are nasty words." He inclined his head to get a better look. "I have seen a lot worse, but I've never seen them embroidered so neatly. Is this why you and Peggy thought Maisie had killed Lyla?"

"Wouldn't you?"

"Maisie was a suspect. Until Kim came forward with her confession." He took a sip of his wine. "Between you and me, her confession doesn't sit right with me. She's not giving us the full details of what she did, but she's adamant it was her. She's refusing to accept legal help too."

"What are you going to do about her?" I settled back on the sofa and cradled my glass.

"We'll be asking her more questions. For now, she's in custody. A night in the cells usually gives people plenty of time to think about their actions. I'm hoping Kim will give us more information in the morning."

"Do you think she's covering up for someone?"

"Such as?"

"Maisie."

He gave me a wry smile. "Is that what Peggy thinks?"

"She does."

His smile faded, and he gave me a look full of concern. "Karis, as much as I admire Peggy, it concerns me how eager she is to get involved in murder cases. And how she gets you involved too. I'm worried you'll get hurt one of these days."

I shifted in my seat under his intense look. "I get myself involved. You know what my psychic visions are like. They come to me for a reason, whether I want them or not."

"I know. But that doesn't stop me from worrying about you."

"You don't need to. I can take care of myself." I took a big drink of my wine. I didn't want to admit that I liked him being concerned about me. I didn't even want to admit that to myself.

Seb put his glass down and reached into his pocket. "I nearly forgot. I've got Erin's rings here. Would you mind returning them to her, please? I won't get the chance to call on her until late tomorrow, and I think she'll be eager to get these back. I was going to give them to Robbie, but he'd already left the station." He handed me a bag with the two rings in it.

"Don't you need these as evidence?"

"No. Kim confessed to stealing them just before admitting to Lyla's murder. Obviously, Lyla's murder takes precedence. But if Erin wants to make a charge against Kim, then she can do. And if we need the rings back, we know where to find them." He gave me a smile which made my heart flutter just the tiniest bit. He said, "Returning these rings is at my discretion. I know Erin's got enough on her mind with her pregnancy. She doesn't need to be stressed about her rings as well."

"Thank you. I know she'll appreciate it. Did Kim say why she'd stolen them?"

"Yes. Lyla told her to." He picked up his wine. "Do you remember that incident at school between Maisie and Lyla? Where Lyla accused her of stealing a necklace?"

"I do."

"Kim told me it wasn't true, which we suspected anyway. Lyla told Kim to back up her accusation in front of everyone at school, and that's what she did."

"Why would she do that?"

He heaved a sigh. "You know how stupid people can be at school. And what they'll do to impress others, no matter who gets hurt."

I knew he was referring to the incident between us which had happened years ago. As far as I was concerned, it was in the past. I said, "But how did Lyla know Erin's rings were in the kitchen?"

"She didn't. When Maisie came into the café on your craft evening, Lyla wanted to get rid of her immediately. She told Kim to find something belonging to you or Erin and to plant it on Maisie. It was only by chance that Kim found those rings in a teapot."

I frowned. "But nothing happened that night. Kim stole the rings but didn't plant them on Maisie."

Seb nodded. "Kim told me she couldn't do it. She claims she saw Lyla in a new light that evening, and didn't like what she saw. And she said that incident led to an argument the next day with her and Lyla, which resulted in her killing Lyla. That's all the information she's prepared to give us."

"It doesn't make sense."

"No, but it will when we get the full details. Shall we talk about something other than murder?" He smiled. "We always seem to be talking about murder or our work, don't we?"

"Not always." I returned his smile. "Tell me how your house-hunting is going. Have you found anything yet? Or are you going to stay living with your mum and dad forever?"

He laughed. "I'll admit that I do like living with my parents. Mum loves cooking for me, and Dad is always doing my washing. I think they like having me back home. But I'm a grown man, and I must make my own way in the world. I must be independent." He raised his glass and gave me a firm nod. "I have seen a couple of houses which could be suitable. Would you mind coming with me to look at them?"

"Me?"

"Yes, you."

"Why me?"

"Because I value your opinion."

I felt my cheeks warming up. "Okay. I'd like that. Thanks."

"Good. Perhaps after the viewings, we could go for a bite to eat somewhere."

Had he just asked me out on a date? More heat flooded my cheeks. I was turning into a human volcano. I'd erupt if I wasn't careful. "That sounds nice."

He drained his glass and put it on the table. "I'd better get going. Dad waits up until I'm home." He stood up and I did too. "I'll let you know how things go with Kim. But if you get any further feelings or visions, let me know."

"I will." I walked him to the door. "Thanks for Erin's rings."

"You are welcome." To my surprise, he leaned forward and planted a brief kiss on my cheek. I caught a whiff of his aftershave. "Goodnight, Karis."

I watched him walk away. I didn't know what to think about Seb. I did like him; I liked him a lot. But could we really start up a relationship again? Would it be a terrible thing if we did?

I shook my head at my thoughts and closed the door. As I returned to the living room, the damaged pictures caught my attention. It was like they were mocking me with an unspoken message. Whatever the message was, it wasn't getting through to me.

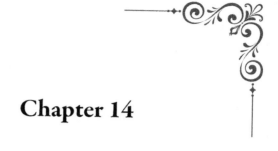

Chapter 14

The strangest feeling came over me the next morning. As soon as I woke up, I knew I had to get out of the house. I checked my phone for messages to make sure everyone was in good health. I had no urgent notifications to let me know anyone was in danger, so I presumed everyone was okay. There was a message from Peggy to say she was off visiting one of her sick friends, but that was all.

I got dressed as quickly as I could, and then jumped into my car. I didn't know what the urgency was, or even which way I was supposed to go, but I headed out of the driveway and let my instincts take over.

And that's what they did. It was almost like the car was driving itself. Turn left here. Second exit on the roundabout. Straight on for a while. Then right, second left and right again. I had no idea where I was going, but I didn't like where I was. The area I found myself in was one of the worst in the city. Rusting cars sat on the grass verges. Many houses were boarded up. Gardens were overrun with weeds and assorted rubbish including battered shopping trolleys. Despite the earliness of the day, groups loitered on corners looking mightily suspicious.

Even though I should have been feeling uneasy at where I was, my instincts wouldn't let up, so on I drove. I headed along a less run-down street and stopped outside a house which wasn't boarded up. A woman was standing on the doorstep and having a heated argument with a man who looked like he was trying to force his way onto the property.

The woman was Maisie Abbot.

Sensing her distress, I stopped the car and got out. Neither she nor the man noticed me.

Maisie shouted, "You can clear off! Mum left nothing for you, for any of you! You took enough from her when she was alive. Can't you leave her alone now? Let her rest in peace?"

The man retaliated, "There's still stuff in there I can sell. Move before I make you move."

Maisie planted her hands on her hips. "No, Nick. You're not taking the last few belongings Mum had. She left them to me. And I won't let you in. Go back to prison where you belong."

The man sneered at her. "Think you're too good for the likes of us, don't you? Ashamed of our family name. We all know you changed your name when you ran away. But that doesn't change who you are. You're a Scargrange, and always will be. Nothing can change that. Shift out of the way."

Nick reached out and gave Maisie a shove. I couldn't help myself. I dashed towards the couple. I pushed Nick to the side. Only too late did I realise how big he was. And how many tattoos and scars he had.

His eyes narrowed and his hands curled into fists; huge fists. He swore at me and raised one fist.

Maisie stepped in front of me and faced her brother. "Don't even think it! Lay one finger on my friend and I'll have you back in prison before the end of the day."

Nick let out a nasty laugh. "Your friend? You don't have friends. Not after what happened with that stupid girl at school. What was her name? Liza? Layla? She knew what you were. One of us. A Scargrange. Does your friend here know what you're really like? Should I tell her?" A calculating look came over his face. "If you want me to keep my mouth shut, you'd better let me in Mum's house and take what belongs to me."

Maisie's head dipped a little. "That girl at school, her name was Lyla. And she's dead. She died a few days ago."

He let out a loud guffaw which made me jump. "Ha! You finally did it, Maisie! Good on you. You finally found the guts to get your revenge. You are one of us after all. I'm proud of you, sis."

"I didn't kill her!" Maisie defended herself.

"Oh, yeah. Of course you didn't. Did you get someone to do it for you? Who? Someone I know?" His eyes were full of pure malice. "You'll want me to keep quiet about this, won't you? It's going to cost you."

"You won't get a penny out of me!" Maisie gave him a sudden push which caused him to stumble backwards. "I'm not like you! Any of you. You sent Mum to an early grave, and you won't get your hands on the few things she left to me. You'd better clear off before I tell the police about those other crimes they don't know about."

"You wouldn't dare." He tried to look defiant, but there was a hint of doubt in his voice.

"I would dare. You mean nothing to me. Nothing. Clear off before I phone the police."

He cast her an evil look before skulking away.

When he'd gone, Maisie's shoulders dropped and she wavered on her feet. Thinking she was going to faint, I put my hands on her arms.

She turned to face me. "Karis, I'm so sorry you had to see that. What must you think of me?"

"Are you okay? Did he hurt you?" I removed my hands.

"I can deal with my brother. I didn't even know Nick was out of prison." She glanced towards the open door. "I would invite you in, but there's nowhere to sit. And I don't have any tea to offer you. Mum must have sold her furniture off over the years. Or someone sold it for her. I feel so bad about leaving her alone for so long. She had to deal with so much. As soon as her house is cleared of her few belongings, I'm leaving this town. I thought I could stay, but my past keeps catching up with me."

"I can understand that. Is there anything I can do to help?"

She gave me a sad smile. "No, thank you. Why are you here?"

I shrugged and lied, "I was in the area and saw you were in trouble."

"I'm glad you turned up. Nick might have turned violent if you hadn't. He's done that before." She shot a nervous glance along the street. In a quieter tone, she said, "Have you heard? About Kim Webb? She's confessed to killing Lyla."

"I did hear. How do you know?"

A noise came from inside the house. "That's my phone. I should get it. It could be the clearance company. If things get sorted out today, I can leave this town for good." She gave me a quick smile before hurrying into her house, firmly closing the door behind her.

As I drove away, two thoughts came to me. Or rather, two questions.

How did Maisie know about Kim's confession?

And why was Maisie Abbot keen to leave town in such a hurry?

Chapter 15

I headed to the café. I arrived there twenty minutes later and found Erin in the kitchen.

"You're early," she said. "I thought I'd be the only one here for a while. I couldn't sleep a wink last night because of these two." She rested her hand on her stomach and smiled. "I can't wait to see them."

"I can't either, but I don't want to see them until they're fully cooked, if you know what I mean."

Her nose wrinkled. "Yuk, but I do know what you mean. Can I get you a cuppa? I was just about to put the kettle on."

"I'll do it. But first, I've got something for you." I handed her the rings. "Seb brought them to my house last night."

Her face lit up. "My rings! He found them! Where?"

"It's a bit of a story. Let me put the kettle on."

I did so, and then told her about Kim stealing her rings. I also told her about my visit to the jewellers which led to the rings. "I'm sorry I couldn't bring them back earlier, but I thought Seb should have them as evidence."

She smiled. "I understand. You're always talking about Seb these days."

"I am not!"

"Yeah, you are. You like him. A lot."

I made a weird noise which was a cross between a har-rumph and a phfft.

"Nonsense. I respect him as a policeman, that's all."

She chuckled. "Whatever you say." She tried to put her rings on. "Oh! Come on. Get on my sausage fingers."

"Erin, don't force them on. Put them somewhere safe." I looked around the kitchen. "Is there somewhere safe in here?"

"Ah, now you're asking. Let me show you what my wonderful husband did for me." She headed over to a photograph of the café which had been taken during its renovation. She took it off the wall and announced, "Ta-da!"

I moved closer. "Is that a wall safe? How long has it been there?"

"About two hours. Robbie installed in early this morning. I told him we didn't need one as I could use the cash safe, but he said this one was just for my belongings. Isn't he sweet? And just in time too. I can keep my rings nearby all day." She placed her rings inside the safe and sighed happily.

I didn't point out the obvious. Robbie worked with Seb and must have known the rings had been recovered. And it was no coincidence he installed this safe so quickly. He must have known I was going to give Erin her rings back today. He was so thoughtful, and yet devious at the same time. How had he managed to keep the information about the recovered rings from Erin?

Erin turned to look at me, her face creased in confusion. "It's weird how Robbie installed the safe this morning." I could almost see the cogs in her head working things out.

I quickly changed the subject. "Did you hear the café door opening? I think we've got our first customers of the day. Shall I see to them?"

Her face was still wrinkled up as she closed the safe and put the photograph back. "No, I'll do it." She walked out of the kitchen. I knew she was going to make the connection soon. Should I warn Robbie?

Before I could think about that, I got a loud buzzing in my ears. The floor seemed to tilt beneath me. I was getting a vision. I held onto the back of the nearest chair and closed my eyes.

My vision began.

I saw Kim Webb sneaking into the kitchen. I could hear voices coming from the main café area. Peggy's voice amongst others. It must have been the night of the cross stitch event.

Kim was looking around the kitchen as if searching for something. She opened a few cupboards, looked inside and moved on. Her glance alighted on the teapot where Erin had put her rings. She lifted the lid. Her eyebrows shot up. She reached inside and took the rings out.

A voice called, "What are you doing?" It was Maisie.

Kim shoved the rings in her pocket. "Nothing." She lowered her head and attempted to leave the kitchen.

Maisie put her hand out and stopped her. "Tell me what you've done, Kim. You're up to something. I know you are."

Keeping her head low, Kim muttered, "You don't know anything."

In a kinder tone, Maisie continued, "I do know. We used to be friends, remember? Before Lyla came between us. And whatever happened in the past, I never blamed you for it."

Kim lifted her head and gave Maisie a searching look. "Really? Even after what I said about you in school?"

"I know Lyla forced you to do it. It wasn't your idea."

Kim's shoulders sagged. "I'm so sorry. I've never apologised to you, Maisie. And I should have. I didn't know how much Lyla's lies would hurt you. I was stupid."

"You were young. But you're not young now. Why are you still friends with Lyla? You must know what she's like by now."

Kim sighed. "I do. She's never changed her ways." She pulled the rings out and showed them to Maisie. "She wanted me to steal something and then blame it on you."

Maisie shook her head. "Why is she like this? Why does she hate me so much?"

"Some people are just like that. It makes them feel better when others are in pain. Even me, and I'm supposed to be her friend."

Maisie put her hand on Kim's shoulder. "I heard about your fiancé. Lyla bragged about it to me when I was unlucky enough to be on the same cruise ship as her. She said he was better off with her, and that he was far too good for you."

"She said that?"

Maisie nodded.

Kim's features hardened. "Someone needs to teach Lyla Gibson-Smith a lesson."

Maisie gave her a small smile. "Do you need my help with that?"

The vision faded. I opened my eyes.

Were Maisie and Kim responsible for Lyla's death? Had they done it together? Or had it been just one of them?

Kim had confessed to the murder. But what if she knew it was Maisie who had done it? Had she confessed to atone for the guilt she felt about Maisie's schooldays?

If so, was Maisie going to get away with murder?

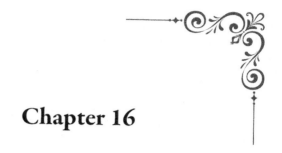

Chapter 16

E rin came back into the kitchen and declared, "He knew! Robbie knew my rings had been found. That's why he installed this safe! Karis, he must have known, mustn't he?"

I shrugged. I didn't want to get involved in her marital arguments.

Erin reached for her phone. "Why didn't he tell me they'd been found? He knew how upset I was." Tears sprang to her eyes. "He lied to me. He's never lied to me before. Why would he do that?"

I gently took the phone from her hand and sat her down. "He didn't lie. He merely kept the truth from you for a while. Maybe Seb asked him to do it. If that was the case, Robbie wouldn't have had an option, would he? Not if your rings were part of a police investigation. Think about it."

Erin muttered, "Stupid police. Stupid investigation."

"If Robbie knew your rings had been recovered, don't you think he would have been eager to let you know, and to get them back to you?"

"Maybe." She sniffed and wiped a tear away.

"And don't you think he would have argued with Seb about letting you know?"

A small smile came to her face. "Probably. I can just imagine him doing that."

"Robbie loves you more than anyone else in the world. He would do anything to keep you happy. Especially in your delicate condition." I grinned at her.

She grinned back. "I am in a delicate condition. He calls me his precious flower. Amongst other things." She blushed and looked down at her hands. "I'll phone him and tell him I've got my rings back." She looked at me and frowned. "You look weird. Did something happen?"

I was tempted to tell her about my vision, but then changed my mind. She didn't need any further upset. "Nothing happened. I'll leave you in peace to talk to your husband. Is it busy in the café?"

"No, not yet. Karis, you don't have to work here every day. You don't even get paid. You still refuse to take a wage, and you know how I feel about that."

"I get a share of the profits. That's enough for me. Anyway, I like working here and talking to people."

"You need to get out more. Have some adventures." She waggled her eyebrows. "Have some romance. You're not quite past it yet."

I sighed. "I feel like it."

"That's rubbish, and you know it. Go home. Get a life."

"Are you trying to get rid of me?"

"Yes, but only because I care about you." She glanced at her stomach. "Once these two come along, I'm going to need your help. But until then, you don't need to be around me so much. I know you like looking after me, but I'm okay." She looked my way and gave me a kind smile. "Why don't you book a holiday? I thought you and Lorrie were planning one."

"We are. I'm not sure how far she's got with the arrangements." The sudden thought of getting away for a week or two appealed to me. But I wasn't going to leave the café that easily. "I'll do a few hours here, and then I'll go home and get a life." I gave her a swift kiss on her cheek. "Phone your husband and tell him how much you love him."

Her eyes shone with mischief. "I'll be telling him a lot more than that."

I held my hand up. "Wait until I'm out of earshot."

I left her to make her call and headed into the café. There were only a few customers and their orders had already been taken. Over the next few hours, the café filled up and I was kept busy. Members of staff came in at various intervals and there was less work for me to do. I decided it was time to leave when Erin bustled over to me with my handbag, grabbed me firmly by the arm and marched me to the door. She gave me a quick hug before passing me my handbag and forcing me into the street.

It was a good job I loved her so much.

She was right about me getting a life. I knew I should do that. But how did I start? It was alright Erin talking about having an adventure, but what if I was too scared to have an adventure on my own?

You're being a wimp, I told myself as I drove home. Woman up, and sort yourself out.

With that determination in mind, I arrived home and marched inside expectedly as if my new life was waiting for me in the living room. I immediately phoned Lorrie with the intention of talking about our holiday. I wanted to get things finalised. To book the tickets. To mark the dates on my calendar. To go shopping for clothes.

She didn't answer. That wasn't unusual because she was at work. She could be in a meeting. I left her a message. Then I put the kettle on and reached for a packet of biscuits. I was going to need subsistence if I was making lots of plans. I took my drink and snack into the living room. Before I sat down, I remembered those small kits which Anita had given me on the craft evening. I could make a start on them while waiting for Lorrie to phone me back.

I took the kits from the drawer where I'd put them and looked at them once more. They were only small and wouldn't take me long to do. I smiled, thinking of myself as an expert now.

I sat on the sofa and considered which one I should do first. The Eiffel Tower looked straightforward. Lots of straight lines and not too much detail. I opened the pack and took the fabric out.

Out of nowhere, a sudden feeling of crushing disappointment flooded me. I gasped and my hand went to my chest. My breath caught in my throat and I felt like someone had put a heavy weight on my shoulders. It was weighing me down. The disappointment was followed by immense sadness. I burst into tears.

As suddenly as they started, my tears stopped. I stared at the cross stitch material on my knee. Was this the cause of my anguish? I picked the bundle of threads up, and once more, sorrow washed through me. I flung the fabric and threads to one side. I wiped my eyes. What was happening? Why was I feeling like this?

Warily, I picked up the cross stitch which had a picture of the Colosseum on the front. I carefully opened it as if disarming a bomb. As soon as my fingers touched the fabric, those awful feelings attacked me again. Fresh tears rolled down my cheeks as wave after wave of dismay rolled over me. It was followed by regret and dull acceptance.

Thoughts were whirring through my brain. I tried to make sense of them. I stiffened as one thought came to me clearly.

I knew I was never going to travel to these places. Never.

I rubbed my forehead. Why was I thinking this? Why?

My hand dropped from my forehead.

Lorrie!

It must be something to do with Lorrie!

My hand shook as I phoned her again.

No answer.

My unease tripled.

I phoned the company she worked for. I don't know how I kept my voice steady as I asked to be put through to Lorrie.

Unaware of my turmoil, the woman replied, "I'm sorry, but Ms Booth hasn't come into the office today. Can I put you through to someone else in her department?"

"Do you know why she hasn't come in?" I could hear my voice becoming louder.

"No, but I'm sure someone in her department could help you. Shall I put you through?"

"Yes, thank you."

My palms were sweating now. Something was wrong with my daughter.

I spoke to three more people in an attempt to find out where Lorrie was. No one knew. How could they not know? The last person I spoke to thought Lorrie hadn't been well the previous day and could have been taking a day off sick. They offered to put me through to Human Resources who would know if she'd phoned in ill.

It was at this point that I burst into tears again. I ended the call and the phone slipped from my hand.

Lorrie's beautiful face came to me. My little girl. I had to see her.

I jumped to my feet. I swayed as my vision blurred.

Then the carpet came up to meet me.

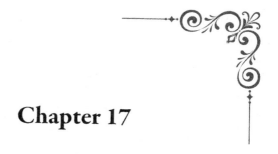

Chapter 17

When I came around, I was sitting on the sofa with my head resting on a man's chest. His arm was around my shoulder and he was pressing something cold against my forehead. I didn't panic as I knew who it was.

I looked up and said, "Seb, what are you doing here?" I frowned. "How did you get in? Wasn't I just on the floor? How long was I there?" I sat up straighter and Seb's arm fell from my shoulders.

He removed the cold compress from my forehead. "You fainted. You were lying on the carpet." His voice caught in his throat. "I thought for a moment you were dead. I was ready to knock your front door down, but it was unlocked. Are you okay? Why did you faint?"

"I...I...Lorrie! Seb, something is wrong with Lorrie!" I tried to get up, but he gently restrained me. "I have to phone her. I have to go to her house. Let me up!"

"What's wrong with her?"

I waved my hand at the discarded cross stitch kits. "The Eiffel Tower! The Colosseum! I got a feeling! Something is terribly wrong. I just know it." I tried to get up again, but Seb's hold on my arm was too strong.

"Karis, you need to calm down. Tell me everything."

"We don't have time! She's in danger. She didn't turn up to work. No one knows where she is. She's not answering her phone." I choked on my words. "Seb, I have to find her."

"Leave this to me. Where does she live?" I answered him. He took his phone out and made some calls. While he did that, I tried to calm myself down. But it was impossible. My little girl needed me right now.

Seb finished his call. "I've got two cars heading to her house. The first one will be there in a few minutes." He took my trembling hands in his. "We'll know what's going on with her very soon. Can you tell me exactly what you experienced? And what have your feelings about Lorrie got to do with the Eiffel Tower?"

I did my best to tell him what had happened. My stupid tears kept falling as I spoke, but I couldn't control them. I concluded, "I feel so annoyed. But I don't know why. Disappointed and annoyed. And angry too. Why would I be angry with Lorrie?"

Seb's phone rang. He answered it, muttered a bit, and then handed the phone to me. "It's your daughter. She's furious."

I grabbed the phone. "Lorrie! Are you alright? Are you hurt? Where are you?"

"Mum? What are you doing on a police phone? Oh, hang on. Have these police officers anything to do with you? The ones who've burst into my bedroom? Mum, what's happened?"

My shoulders sagged in relief. "You're okay."

"I'm not okay! I had a late night out with my friends and was having a lovely lie-in until I was rudely interrupted by these policemen. It's not the best way to be woken up." Her voice lowered and I could almost see her smile. "Although, one of them is rather cute."

"Oh, Lorrie." I laughed in relief at her words. "You are okay, though? Is everything alright? You didn't answer your phone. I phoned your work number, and they didn't know where you were. I panicked."

"They knew I was taking a day off. I booked it last week. Idiots. Mum, why were you so worried? Did you have a vision about me? Is there something I should know?"

"No, love. It was just a feeling I had." My attention went to the kits on the carpet. "To be honest, I don't even know if my feelings were linked to you. I just assumed. But you are okay, aren't you?"

She laughed. "A banging headache, but that's all. I'll come around later and make you a meal. We can talk about our holiday. I've been looking at hotels. I want your opinion before I book them."

"We're still going on holiday?"

"Of course we are! Mum, is everything okay with you?"

"Yes. Just being an anxious mother. I'm glad you're safe. I love you."

"I love you too. I'll see you later. Stop worrying so much. Bye."

I gave the phone back to Seb.

He smiled. "She sounds just like you when she's annoyed. The officers heard her phone ringing inside her house, but she didn't answer the door. They had to break it down. I'll make sure it's repaired immediately."

"Thank you so much for doing that. Will you get into trouble because of it? It was hardly a police matter."

"It mattered to me, and I'm a police officer." He smiled at me. "Let's have a cup of tea. Then you can tell me more about what you experienced with these kits." His smiled faded. "I've got a feeling these have something to do with Lyla's death."

"Oh? Are you becoming psychic now?"

He tapped his head. "I knew you were going to say those exact words, Karis. I just knew it." He gave me a long look. "There's something else, isn't there? You've had another vision. Am I right?"

My eyes widened. "You are right."

He stood up. "Stay right there. I'll be back with the tea in a minute."

I asked, "Why did you come here anyway? Was there something you wanted to tell me?"

His shrug was casual. "I was just driving past and saw your car in the driveway. Just wanted to make sure you were okay." He left the room.

I settled back on the sofa. It was nice to have someone care about me. I wasn't used to it, but I liked it. I rested my head back and closed my eyes. Now that I'd stopped panicking about Lorrie, I could analyse my previous feelings which those kits had caused me to have.

I did so and tried to make sense of them.

Slowly, they began to make sense.

I opened my eyes. I didn't like where my thoughts had landed.

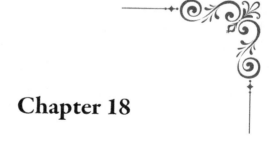

Chapter 18

Over the next hour, Seb and I discussed Lyla's murder investigation and where my visions had led us. He made a call to someone at his office, and then we set off in his car. I took some items with me.

We entered Hart's Haberdashery soon after.

Anita was behind the counter serving a customer. We waited until the customer had left, her bag stuffed with wool and patterns.

Anita cast us a smile. "Hi, Karis. It's good to see you again." Her smile dropped when she looked at Seb. "Oh, DCI Parker. I didn't think I'd see you again. Has something happened? Have you found out who killed Lyla yet? I'm sorry I couldn't identify those threads for you. I did ask some of my regulars, but no one had heard of that brand. I think Lyla must have bought them online somewhere."

Seb took a step forward. "She did buy them online. We went through her bank records and located a possible shop. They have confirmed Mrs Gibson-Smith bought those threads last month."

Anita nodded. "That's one puzzle solved then." She glanced towards the door behind her. Her voice was quieter as she said, "I still can't believe someone would kill Lyla. I know she had her enemies, but murder is so extreme. I haven't told Mum yet. I don't want to upset her. She didn't know Lyla well, just as a customer. But I know she'll be upset. Is there something I can help you with?"

"Yes. I want to ask you about Maisie Abbot. She changed her name years ago. She used to be called Maisie Scargrange." Seb waited for her response.

"Maisie! Yes, of course. I remember her. She used to work here when she was at school. Helped out on a Saturday, and after school now and again. Such a hard worker. Got on well with Mum. It was Mum who taught Maisie how to do cross stitch. Any spare moment Maisie had, she came here. And who could blame her? She didn't have the best of families." She smiled. "Maisie became part of our family. Mum and I cared deeply for her."

"Did you know she was back in town?" Seb asked.

Anita's eyebrows rose. "Is she? I didn't know that. Do you know where she lives? I'd love to see her again."

I fidgeted with the bag in my hand. I was dreading the moment when I would have to take the contents out.

Seb continued, "Maisie knew Mrs Gibson-Smith. They were at school together. Did you know that?"

Anita nodded. "Maisie didn't talk about her. But I do remember Lyla coming here with that friend of hers, Kim. They didn't buy anything. They followed Maisie around the shop and made fun of her. Mum hated them. She chased them out of the shop a few times, but they kept sneaking back in. To her credit, Maisie ignored them and got on with her work." Comprehension dawned on her face. "Oh! You don't think Maisie had anything to do with Lyla's death, do you? Is that why she's come back to town? But why would she do that after all these years? That doesn't sound like Maisie at all."

Seb hesitated for a fraction before saying, "No, Maisie didn't kill Lyla. We've checked her alibi. Ms Hart, when Maisie worked here, there was a robbery. According to our records, an amount of money was stolen. You reported one thousand pounds was taken. Is that right?"

Anita fiddled with the collar of her dress. "That's right. One thousand pounds. Some came from the till, but most of it was in the safe." She glanced upwards. "I can hear Mum moving about. I must see to her. Was there anything else?"

"Yes. We caught the men who stole your money, Ms Hart. They said they took five thousand pounds from here. They claim it was in your safe."

"What? No, that's not right. We didn't have that much money in the safe." Her laugh which followed was too shrill. "They must be lying. How can you trust thieves?"

Seb went on, "This theft happened at the time when Maisie was working here. Considering who her family were and their reputation, did you suspect Maisie was in on the theft? Perhaps you thought she'd tipped her family off about how much was in the safe."

"No! Never!" Anita backed up a little.

Seb persisted. "She could have known about your safe. She could have known the combination."

Anita shook her head vehemently. "No. I never suspected Maisie. She was like a family member to us. She would never betray us, not after the way we'd treated her. Not when Mum had been so kind to her."

Seb said, "I think you're lying, Ms Hart. I think you did suspect her. Shortly after the theft, Maisie abruptly left town. You must have thought she was running away with her proceeds from the theft here. The five thousand pounds."

"It wasn't five thousand pounds. I've told you that." Her face flushed. "I never suspected Maisie. Never."

Seb looked my way. "Karis. Now, please."

I moved closer to Anita and placed the damaged cross stitch pictures on the counter, the ones which had been hanging on the walls of the shop. I said, "I think you made these, not Lyla. I found these messages about Maisie written underneath the stitches."

Anita stared silently at the pictures.

I pressed on. "I think you hated Maisie. You must have suspected she had something to do with the thefts. She betrayed you. And your mum. It's understandable you would hate her. Did you put these on your wall to remind yourself how much you hated her? To stop you from trusting anyone ever again?"

She remained silent.

I brought out some other items. "These are the kits you gave me on the craft evening. I think you were going to visit these places. I think you were saving money so you could go travelling one day. That would explain the five thousand pounds. But you told the police it was one thousand because you didn't want your mum to know you'd been saving money for your travels. Maybe you thought she wouldn't let you go. Is that right?"

The smallest of smiles alighted on her face. "I've always wanted to travel. Always. I'd made plans. I had a list of where I was going first."

I nodded. "But that theft affected your mum badly, didn't it? She must have suspected Maisie too. That would have destroyed her. You couldn't leave her alone while you went on holiday. You couldn't even leave her for a few hours the other evening."

"She needs me nearby. All the time." She looked up from the kits. "She fell to pieces when Maisie left. Her heart was broken. She could barely function. How could I leave her? Even for a few days?"

I asked, "Did you both think Maisie was to blame for the theft?"

"Not at first. We didn't believe she was capable of such a thing, such a betrayal. She wouldn't treat us that way." Her face twisted in hate. "But then Lyla and her friend came in here shortly after the theft. Lyla said Maisie had been planning to steal from us for months. She said they had laughed about it at school. Maisie had only pretended to like working here. It was all part of the plan she'd come up with. Lyla gloated about how she was best friends with Maisie, and they'd only pretended otherwise to fool me and Mum. I believed her. Mum did too. That's when I started to hate Maisie. I detested her. I could barely eat some days because I was full of hate."

I said, "I think you discovered the truth about Maisie recently. When was that?"

"It was on the day after your craft evening. Lyla brought those photographs in of her holidays. I saw Maisie in the background. I saw how she was in a uniform. I asked Lyla about her. I wondered if they were still friends." Anger infused Anita's face and she placed her hands flat down on the counter. "She laughed. She had the nerve to laugh at my questions. Then the truth came out. Lyla had lied about Maisie being part of the robbery. She even knew who had really committed it, but had never told me despite coming to my shop many times over the years. Do you know what she said?"

I shook my head.

"She said it was in Maisie's nature to steal, and that she probably would have stolen from us one day. She claimed she did us a favour by saying Maisie was to blame for the theft. And she believed it! She truly believed it! Because of her lies, Mum had a breakdown. I wasn't able to leave her. I never went on holiday. I never saw the Eiffel Tower. Or any of the other places. And it was all because of Lyla and her nasty lies. I couldn't let her get away with it. I just couldn't. You do understand, don't you?"

I gave her a small nod. I did understand her disappointment and anger because I'd experienced them. But I couldn't understand how she thought killing Lyla was justified.

Anita gave me a direct look and the coldness in her eyes startled me. "You should have seen her face when she knew she was dying. I went to her house on the pretence of giving her some free samples. I saw that kit she was working on. I made some excuse for needing a glass of water, and then I poisoned the thread. And the cloth. I wanted to make sure the poison got into her. I even stayed with her a while to make sure it worked. It was worth it to see the look in her eyes."

I looked away. I couldn't bear to see the triumph on her face.

Seb said something to Anita before using his phone. Then he touched my arm and said, "I'll take it from here. Once my officers arrive, I'll drive you home."

"It's okay. I'll walk. I need the fresh air."

I quickly left the shop which Peggy had described as a piece of heaven.

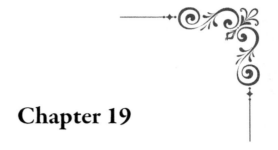

Chapter 19

I was nearly home when I heard someone calling my name.

It was Peggy. She was waiting at the bus stop, carrying a couple of bags.

My heart felt heavy. I would have to tell her about Anita.

"I saw you when I was on the bus," Peggy said. "Are you out for a walk?"

I took one of the bags from her. I didn't know how to begin. I said, "How are your friends at the hospital?"

We proceeded to walk along.

"They're fine. They seem a bit better today. I popped to that supermarket opposite the hospital for a few bits and pieces. I thought I could make us a fish pie for dinner."

"You don't have to keep making meals for me," I said with a smile.

"But I like doing it. It's better than cooking for one."

We walked on for a bit in silence.

Peggy suddenly stopped walking and turned to face me. "Okay, what is it? There's something wrong. What's happened?"

"I don't want to tell you here. Let's go to my house and put the kettle on."

"It's something bad, isn't it?"

I nodded.

"You've found out who killed Lyla, haven't you?"

I nodded again. I took a deep breath and said, "It was Anita."

Peggy stared at me.

I went on, "She admitted it. Seb and I went to her shop and talked to her."

Peggy shook her head slowly. "No. That can't be right. Not Anita. I've been going to her shop for years. She wouldn't do something like that." She looked at the pavement, still shaking her head. "Not Anita."

I took the other bag from her. "I'll tell you everything when we get home." I put both carrier bags in one hand and put my free hand on Peggy's elbow. Without saying another word, we headed towards my house.

Lorrie was standing by my front door about to let herself in. She turned when she heard us approach. "Hi Mum! I thought I would turn up a bit early. Hello, Peggy. How are you?" Her cheerful smile vanished. "Peggy? You don't look good. What's wrong?"

"She's in shock," I told Lorrie. "Let's get her inside."

It took us a few minutes to settle Peggy in the living room. Her forehead was creased as if trying to make sense of my words. I placed a cup of tea in her hands and sat at her side. While she sipped it, I quickly told Lorrie about Lyla and my visions. I ended by telling them both about Anita's confession.

Lorrie listened with her mouth hanging open. "Mum, you should start working for the police. How many murders have you got involved with now?"

"Too many." I turned to Peggy. "I didn't want to believe it was Anita either, but she admitted it."

"It's so sad, so very sad," Peggy said. "All those years I've been going to her shop and I never knew the hate she was nursing. I knew her mum hadn't been well for years, but I had no idea her problems had stopped Anita from living her life. And all because of Lyla and her malicious lies. People just don't realise the harm their careless words can cause."

Lorrie said, "I'm confused. If the police caught the thieves years ago, why didn't they tell Anita and her mum? Then they would have known it had nothing to do with Maisie. They could have stopped hating her."

I shrugged. "I don't know the answer to that."

Peggy lifted her head and looked towards the window. "We know a man who might. Isn't that Seb's car pulling up outside?"

Lorrie strained her neck. "Seb? Do you mean DCI Parker? I haven't met him yet, but I've heard you both talk about him. What's he doing here?"

"He calls on your mum all the time," Peggy advised her. "No matter the time of day. He's always here."

"He is not," I argued. I stood up and opened the front door before Seb could knock.

He said, "How are you? I wanted to make sure you got home okay."

"I'm fine. Come in. Lorrie's here. And Peggy."

"I don't want to intrude."

"You're not. Lorrie wants to meet you anyway." That was a bit of a lie but I knew my daughter well. She would be eager to know what Seb was like. Nosiness runs in our family.

He straightened his tie and suddenly looked nervous. He came inside and followed me through to the living room. Peggy and Lorrie had their heads together and were whispering something. They were probably talking about Seb.

They both looked up guiltily when they heard us approach. Lorrie stood up and beamed at Seb. "Hi! I'm Lorrie. We spoke on the phone earlier after you sent those friends of yours to break into my house."

Seb blanched. "Oh. Yes. Right. Sorry. I didn't mean to cause you distress. Sorry."

Lorrie laughed. "I wasn't distressed. I know how worried Mum gets about me. It was kind of you to do that. And having two handsome men break into my house eager to find me is going to make an excellent story."

Peggy gave Seb a narrow-eyed look. "Why haven't you sent any handsome policemen to break into my house? What's wrong with me?"

Seb swallowed. I felt sorry for him and said, "Leave him alone. Seb, would you like a cup of tea?"

He gave me a grateful smile. "No, thank you. I've got a lot to do at the station. I wanted to make sure you got home safely."

Peggy said, "You could have phoned her."

"I think it's nice that he came here," Lorrie said. She looked at Seb. "Didn't you and Mum used to date? Years and years ago?"

I began to feel uncomfortable. Seb was about to be interrogated by my nosy daughter.

Instead of being embarrassed, there was a touch of pride in Seb's voice as he replied, "We did. I was the envy of all the boys at school." He smiled at me.

I smiled back at him, feeling years younger.

Peggy stood up and came over to us. "If I'm not interrupting you two, I want to know why the police didn't tell Anita they'd found the real thieves. Why didn't they? I thought they were supposed to do that. If they had, none of this would have happened. Well? What have you got to say to that?"

Seb answered, "I had the same question myself. I phoned the station and they spoke to the officer who had arrested the culprits. After the arrest, he did visit Hart's Haberdashery. He spoke to Anita's mum and gave her all the details."

"Oh." Peggy looked taken aback. "When was this?"

"Ten years ago. The officer also told her how much was stolen."

Peggy moved back to the sofa and sat down. "Anita's mum knew and she said nothing to Anita? I don't understand. Why would she do that?"

I said, "Maybe she wanted to keep Anita at home with her. She could have worked out what the extra money was for."

"But that's so cruel. If she knew Anita wanted to travel, she should have encouraged her to do so." Peggy's hand went to her chest. "Now I know why Anita didn't want to join in with my stitch-along. I told her I was going to do a map of the world and asked if she wanted to do the project too. But she said no because she hadn't been anywhere. She laughed about it, but her heart must have been breaking. Poor love."

"She's not a poor love," I pointed out. "She murdered Lyla."

"I know," Peggy said. "But it needn't have happened. Why did Kim confess to the murder? Have you asked her yet?"

Seb nodded. "Kim thought Maisie had done it. It was her way of apologising to Maisie for the hurt she'd caused her in the past. We're not sure if we're going to charge her with wasting police time yet, or for the theft of Erin's rings. I'm going to deal with those matters later."

Peggy's eyes brimmed with tears. "None of this should have happened."

Lorrie sat next to Peggy and put her arm around her shoulders. "Bad things happen sometimes. And there's nothing we can do about them. Peggy, I'm going to make Mum a meal tonight. I'd love it if you could join us."

Peggy said, "I was going to make her a meal too. What did you have in mind?"

"I hadn't thought that far. I was going to drive to the shops later and see if inspiration strikes me."

Peggy brightened a little. "I've got the ingredients for a fish pie. And an apple crumble. We could make it together."

"Great. Let's do that. Shall we make a start now? I've brought some wine with me. I know it's early, but one or two glasses won't hurt."

"I never say no to wine." Peggy looked at Seb. "You can stay too. You've practically moved in anyway."

"I shall ignore your last comment," Seb said. "I'm afraid I can't stay for dinner as I'll be working late tonight. But thank you for the kind offer. I'll be off now. Nice to meet you, Lorrie."

"You too."

I followed Seb out of the house and over to his car. He leaned against it and said, "I've set up some house viewings for this weekend. Would you still be able to come with me?"

I looked into his eyes and felt a twinge of excitement. And it wasn't related to seeing houses. "I would love that. And I'll take you for lunch afterwards. My treat."

He grinned. "You're on. Karis, you do know that Peggy and Lorrie have their faces pressed up against your window, don't you?"

I nodded. "I can sense them. Let's give them something to look at." I moved forward and gave him a kiss on his lips.

"What was that for?"

"For believing my visions. For watching out for me. For just being here. I could get used to it."

He gave me a long look. "I could too. I'll phone you later." He looked towards my house and waved at the peeping Toms. "Bye you two!" He gave me another smile before getting in his car and driving away.

As I watched him go, I tried to analyse my feelings about him. But I gave up. Some feelings are impossible to analyse.

About the author

I live in a county called Yorkshire, England with my family. This area is known for its paranormal activity and haunted dwellings. I love all things supernatural and think there is more to this life than can be seen with our eyes.

I HOPE YOU ENJOYED this story. If you did, I'd love it if you could post a small review. Reviews really help authors to sell more books. Thank you!

THIS STORY HAS BEEN checked for errors by myself and my team. If you spot anything we've missed, you can let us know by emailing us at: april@aprilfernsby.com

YOU CAN VISIT MY WEBSITE at: www.aprilfernsby.com[1]

MANY THANKS TO Paula Proofreader[2]

———— ❦ ————

WARM WISHES
   April Fernsby

2. https://paulaproofreader.wixsite.com/home

Also by April Fernsby:

———— ⌒◯⌒ ————

THE PSYCHIC CAFÉ MYSTERIES

———— ⌒◯⌒ ————

BOOK 1 - A DEADLY DELIVERY
  Book 2 - A Fatal Wedding
  Book 3 - Tea And Murder
  Book 4 - The Knitting Pattern Mystery

———— ⌒◯⌒ ————

THE BRIMSTONE WITCH Mysteries

———— ⌒◯⌒ ————

BOOK 1 - MURDER OF A Werewolf
  Book 2 - As Dead As A Vampire
  Book 3 - The Centaur's Last Breath
  Book 4 - The Sleeping Goblin
  Book 5 - The Silent Banshee
  Book 6 - The Murdered Mermaid
  Book 7 - The End Of The Yeti
  Book 8 - Death Of A Rainbow Nymph
  Book 9 - The Witch Is Dead
  Book 10 - A Deal With The Grim Reaper
  Book 11 - A Grotesque Murder
  Book 12 - The Missing Unicorn

———— ⌒◯⌒ ————

SIGN UP TO MY NEWSLETTER and I'll let you know about my new releases and special offers:

www.aprilfernsby.com[3]

FOLLOW ME ON Bookbub[4]

---

3.   http://www.aprilfernsby.com

4. https://www.bookbub.com/authors/april-fernsby

The Cross Stitch Puzzle
A Psychic Café Mystery
(Book 5)
By
April Fernsby
www.aprilfernsby.com
Copyright 2019 by April Fernsby

Don't miss out!

Visit the website below and you can sign up to receive emails whenever April Fernsby publishes a new book. There's no charge and no obligation.

https://books2read.com/r/B-A-LQJE-OJTX

BOOKS 2 READ

Connecting independent readers to independent writers.

Also by April Fernsby

A Brimstone Witch Mystery
As Dead As A Vampire
The Centaur's Last Breath
The Sleeping Goblin
The Silent Banshee
The Murdered Mermaid
The End Of The Yeti
Death Of A Rainbow Nymph
The Witch Is Dead
A Deal With The Grim Reaper
A Grotesque Murder
The Missing Unicorn

A Psychic Cafe Mystery
A Deadly Delivery
Tea and Murder
The Knitting Pattern Mystery
The Cross Stitch Puzzle

Printed in Great Britain
by Amazon